Road to Rimrock

The town of Rimrock lay dying, and its local drunk lay in the gutter, passed out again. As usual, Marshal Matt Stryker put Stan Ruggart in the hoosegow to sleep off the whiskey like a regular lowlife. But Ruggart has a family, and a fortune.

When Ruggart's throat is cut and the will turns up in Stryker's pocket there are serious problems on the horizon. The marshal needs to keep ahead of three gunmen looking for vengeance, and stay alive long enough to probate the will. Two women also want him dead, and one wants to go with him on the road to Rimrock. . . .

Road to Rimrock

Chuck Tyrell

 **A Black Horse Western**

ROBERT HALE · LONDON

© Chuck Tyrell 2012
First published in Great Britain 2012

ISBN 978-0-7090-9632-0

Robert Hale Limited
Clerkenwell House
Clerkenwell Green
London EC1R 0HT

www.halebooks.com

Typeset by
Derek Doyle & Associates, Shaw Heath
Printed and bound in Great Britain by
CPI Antony Rowe, Chippenham and Eastbourne

For WOS, where people know what's important in life

1

The shot came as Marshal Matt Stryker started his midnight rounds of Rimrock. He drew his six-gun and trotted down Washington Way. As he passed the President saloon, he saw a crumpled shape in the shadow of the dilapidated boardwalk in front of what was once Rimrock Mercantile. No more shots.

Stryker knelt by the fallen man. He grasped a shoulder and shook it. No response. Keeping his gun ready, he levered the body over. It smelled of whiskey, and he recognized Stan Ruggart.

Lying face up now, Ruggart began to snore.

'Jayzus,' Stryker muttered. He holstered his Remington, hauled Ruggart up by one arm and levered the limp drunk up and over his left shoulder.

'Ruggart shot, Marshal?' Randall Johnson stood at the batwings of the President. Stan Ruggart was the saloon's best customer.

'Not so's I can tell,' Stryker said, 'but I'll put him in the cell for the night, just in case.'

'Right,' Johnson said. Silence came from inside the President. Business was nowhere near jumping.

Stryker's office stood between a former millinery and a abandoned law office half a block down Washington Way.

He shoved the door open, strode to the simple cell in the corner of the room, and lowered Ruggart to the thin pad on the single bunk. Ruggart mumbled and turned to the wall. Stryker left the cell open. He turned down the coal-oil lamp and sat at the battered oak desk.

The town paid the marshal a hundred a month, but it was a month behind and Stryker doubted it would make this month's payday either. The time to move on had come. Rimrock was dying and Matt Stryker had no intention of staying for the funeral. He settled his black Stetson over his eyes and put his feet on the desk.

Next morning, when the sun got high enough, Stryker thumped on the cell door. 'Get out, Ruggart,' he said.

'Good God, Matt, it ain't even noon yet. How can you expect a drinking man to wake up so early?'

'Out. I only put you in there to save your skinny neck. Be glad you're not dead.'

'Who'd wanna kill me?'

'That's what I'd like to know. Who?'

Ruggart shrugged. 'Dunno. I'm just the town drunk.'

Stryker measured the alcoholic again. Despite the fact that he spent many nights in the Rimrock hoosegow, he never looked down and out. Day old beard, to be sure, but that would soon be gone. Good white shirt and wool vest. Striped California pants. Ruggart looked somewhat dishevelled, but Stryker knew he would be a dandy again by the time he started his day's drinking at the President.

Stryker'd worn the badge in Rimrock, south of the Grand Canyon and east of the Colorado River, for nearly two years. The gold that had launched Rimrock was long gone, and in the year 1879 the town subsisted on three ranches, a half-dozen farms, and the stage run from Winona to Ehrenburg. Hardly enough business to pay a marshal and little need for peacekeeping, except for tossing a drunken Stan Ruggart in the town's single cell when he passed out at his usual table at the President.

'It's all right if I leave, then?' Ruggart asked.

'Sure would like to know who took that shot at you last night,' Stryker said.

Ruggart's face went serious. He pulled a folded paper from an inner pocket in his vest. ' 'Preciate it if you'd keep this for me,' he said, holding the paper out to Stryker.

Stryker glanced at the paper as he unfolded it, then took another look. 'This says you own a quarter of the Dominion Mine.' He read more. 'Registered in Washoe County, Nevada.'

'It does and I do. Owned the whole thing at one time, but sold off three-quarters to Consolidated Mining. British money, I heard. Keeps me in booze,' Ruggart said.

'Jayzus. But this names you. No one could just shoot you and claim your share of the mine.'

'True. Maybe.'

'So what good does it do for me to carry this around for you?'

'Someone's out to kill me, Matt. You know they won't give up with only one try.'

'You could leave Rimrock. Most everybody else's doing that,' Stryker said.

'I like it here,' Ruggart said. 'Mood of the town fits my own. Down and out.'

Stryker gave Ruggart a hard look. 'Stan, if it's the whiskey that's got you down, I can lock you in the cell until you dry out.'

Ruggart grinned. 'Nah. I like whiskey. I don't have to work for money. Don't have to deal with other drunks while I'm in Rimrock. Thanks, Matt, but I'll continue drinking.'

Stryker shrugged. 'Your life, Stan. I can't tell you how to live it.'

The grin stayed on Ruggart's face, but never reached his sad eyes. 'That's right, Matt. My life.'

Ruggart left the marshal's office and walked southeast on Washington Way. Stryker figured he'd head for the hotel, get a bath perhaps, and start his day of drinking a little earlier than usual. After all, the hair of the dog is the best remedy for the aches of the morning after, and Ruggart no doubt had a mountain of aches.

Ruggart stayed on Stryker's mind the whole day, but he was still surprised to see the town drunk in his office when he got back from afternoon rounds.

'Make yourself to home,' Stryker said.

Ruggart looked up. 'I spend enough time in here, Matt. It's like a second home, and a bit less lonely than my room. Besides, the door was wide open.'

Stryker grinned. 'I reckon jail's like a second home to a rock-hard criminal like you. Want me to open up your cell so you can move in?'

A ghost of a smile touched Ruggart's face. 'Not today, Matt.' He held out an envelope. 'Could you hold this with the Dominion shares, please?'

Stryker took the envelope, a question on his face.

'My last will and testament,' Ruggart said.

'You going to war?'

'Who knows when the bullet will come, Matt. It's good to be ready.'

Stryker took the envelope.

'Now, if you will excuse me, I'll go have a drink. It's dry work sitting around this office in the heat of the afternoon.' He tipped his hat. 'By your leave, Marshal.'

Stryker stepped aside to let Ruggart out. 'Stan,' he said, holding up the envelope. 'Who does this go to?'

'No one,' Ruggart said, 'until I die. Then you can open it and see for yourself.'

Stan Ruggart went on living and drinking, Matt Stryker went on making his rounds, and Rimrock went on dying. Then Tom Hall rode in.

Stryker stepped out of the marshal's office as Hall went by. 'Tom Hall,' he called.

Hall reined his appaloosa to a halt. He sat the horse easily with his hands crossed on the saddle horn.

'Figuring on staying long?'

'Depends on how things turn out, Marshal. I could be on my way before sundown, and then again, I might find myself staying for a while.'

'When you turn up, Hall, people tend to die, so let me make one thing clear. If anyone in my town dies while you're here, even if it's from natural causes, the first person I'll look for is you.'

Hall might have smiled. It was hard to tell. 'People naturally hate me,' he said. 'They try to kill me, so if I don't kill them first, I'm dead. I got no hankering to be dead, Matt Stryker, even in your town.'

'You've been warned, Tom Hall. Don't you think I'm kidding either. And don't you think I can't take you.'

A real smile came to Hall's face. 'Now that's a proposition, Stryker. I'm not sure you could take me, but I ain't sure I can take you. What say we steer clear of each other?'

Stryker waved him on and went back inside.

A few minutes later, a cowboy from the Fallen Arch ranch stuck his head in the office door. 'Hey, Marshal,' he said. 'Randy said to tell you Stan Ruggart ain't showed up at the President tonight.'

'Thank ya, Jackie. I'll look into it.'

The cowboy leaped off the porch, bounced up into the saddle of a steeldust gelding, and lit out down Washington Way at a dead run.

Stryker's lips curled slightly. He strapped on his

Remington Army and walked down to the President saloon, which for once was jumping.

'Hey, Randy,' a drinker called as Stryker entered the saloon. 'How come there ain't no doves hereabouts? Man needs a poke once in a while, don't he?'

'How often do you come drinking, Bobby Lee?' Johnson fired his question from behind the bar.

'I been here twice this month already,' Bobby Lee said as if he supported the President with his own custom.

'How many cowboys at the Rocking R?'

'Six, counting the *segundo*.'

'So if you all six come in twice a month and you each had a poke every time, that'd end up twelve pokes for the whole month. Let me tell you, Bobby Lee, there ain't a dirty dove in the territory that could stay alive on twelve pokes a month. That's why there ain't no doves in Rimrock.'

'Shee-it. 'S got so's a man can't get no diversion around here.'

Stryker stepped to the near end of the bar. After the cool air outside, the President felt warm and humid, and smelled of sour beer, spilt whiskey, cowboy sweat, and pine sawdust.

Johnson came down the bar to face Stryker.

'Ruggart's not here?' Stryker asked.

Johnson shook his head. 'Come in for half a bottle or so just after noon, but I ain't seen him tonight. Ain't like him.'

'I'll check the hotel,' Stryker said.

Outside the President the street was dark except for the saloon and a weak light from the Rimrock Hotel. Horses stood hipshot at the hitching rails near the saloon, but the rest of Washington Way was empty. No people. No wagons. No movement of any kind. Even the night air seemed to have a musty unused quality. Stryker took a deep breath. What had happened to Stan Ruggart? He stepped off the porch and walked with a stolid stride toward the hotel, raising ankle-high puffs of dust with each step.

Like the street, the lobby of the Rimrock Hotel was empty. A coal-oil lamp burned low at one end of the counter. The register lay open. Keys hung from pegs within easy reach. 'Sign the book and take a key,' said a sign next to the guest register. Stryker checked the signatures. Ruggart's was last. No one else had checked in since. Stan Ruggart lived in an empty hotel and had done for nearly three months.

Stryker picked up the lamp and climbed the stairs. Once the ground floor had housed a restaurant. Now it lay silent like the rest of the town.

Ruggart often said his room number brought him good fortune. Lucky Seven, he called it. Stryker raised the lamp to check the brass number over the door. No mistake – 7. He tapped on the door. Silence. He knocked. No sound. He banged. No response. He tried the knob, and the door opened.

A step into the room, Stryker raised the lamp high. Ruggart lay on his bed, fully clothed, his eyes wide as if in shock, his mouth open as if crying for help, his throat cut so deep the wound looked like a second mouth.

'Ah shit. Too late.' Stryker covered the body with the spare blanket folded at the foot of the bed and went to look for Tom Hall.

2

Stryker left the lamp on the counter in the lobby. He pulled his Remington Army .44 from its holster, checked the action, added a sixth bullet to its cylinder, returned it to its place on his hip, and hitched the gunbelt to settle it more comfortably. He opened the front door, but stood aside for a moment before stepping through.

'Hold still, Stryker.' The click of a hammer being eared back punctuated the sound of Tom Hall's voice.

Stryker stopped. 'Stan Ruggart's dead,' he said.

'I know.'

'You?'

'No. The stories they tell about me are exaggerated by far.'

'So why are you holding a gun on me?' Stryker started to turn around.

'Stand still, Stryker.'

'OK. Now what?'

'Give me your word you won't drag iron, and we can go to your office to talk.'

'You got it. I'll be interested to hear how you know Stan's dead.'

'Move along. You walk ahead.'

Stryker stepped down from the hotel's wooden porch,

14

preferring the dust of Washington Way to the rotting board-walk. He strode ahead, not checking to see whether Hall followed.

If anything, the ruckus inside the President saloon was louder when Stryker passed. No one noticed the tall man with a star followed by a wiry form that walked out into the street to avoid the lightfall from the saloon's windows.

Sounds from the saloon faded as they neared the marshal's office. 'I'm going to open the door,' Stryker said.

'No lamp yet,' Hall said. 'No reason to take risks.'

Stryker pushed the door open and entered the dark office. He went to the desk, unbuckling his gunbelt while he walked. He brushed a hand along the wall until he located a protruding peg to hang the gun rig on. 'Coming in?' he said.

Tom Hall stepped through the door and pushed a chair back against the far wall. He sat. 'You can close the door,' he said. 'And when you light the lamp, keep it low and on your side of the room.'

Stryker shut the door. 'What's this all about?' He felt along the shelf behind his desk until he found the coal-oil lamp.

Hall said nothing.

Scraping a match alight with his thumbnail, Stryker lifted the lamp's chimney and lit its wick. The feeble pool of light thrown by the lamp hardly reached Stryker's desk. He sat in his chair. 'OK,' he said. 'What's going on?'

'You seen a Wanted poster on me, Stryker?'

'No.'

'You won't. Because I always take care not to break the law.'

'Then why cut Stan's throat?'

'I told you. It wasn't me.'

'And I heard you. Not sure I believe you, though.'

'OK. I came here looking for Stan Ruggart . . .'

Stryker's eyebrows rose.

'. . . but not to kill him. I was hired to protect him. Got here too late.'

'Who bought you?'

'Can't say,' Hall said. 'Gave my word.'

Stryker said nothing.

'Pisses me off somewhat,' Hall said, 'that some sneak in the night killed the man I shoulda protected.'

Stryker said nothing.

'Know any knife men?'

Stryker said nothing.

'You don't want to find that cutter?'

'I'll find him . . . or her,' Stryker said.

'May sound strange, Stryker, but I'd like to tag along.'

The room lapsed into silence. Muted sounds of revelry came from the President.

'All right, Tom. You disappear until morning. I'll nose around tonight. See you at breakfast.'

'Where at?'

'Only one place still open. Charlie Stark runs it. The sign says "FOOD". Stryker waved at the far side of the street. 'Over there.'

'OK. You got a bottle?'

'Why?'

'Don't want to show up at that saloon, and it's been a dry ride.'

Stryker opened the bottom drawer of his desk and fished out a bottle of Old Potrero. 'Don't you drink this dry,' he said.

'Put it on the desk,' Hall said, 'and could you take that lamp and go check on the cell in the corner? I'll get out of your way. See you at breakfast.'

Matt rose from the chair, turned away from Hall, picked

up the lamp and, keeping it close to his body, moved toward the cell in the back of the room. He heard only the click of the door catch as Hall left. *Mighty careful man.* After a good ten minutes, Stryker put his gun rig back on, took a sawed-off from the gun rack, and headed for the President.

The bedlam in the President had grown even further. As Matt entered, shotgun in the crook of his arm, at least two dozen men, cowboys by their dress, crowded the room. He sauntered to the near end of the bar and leaned against it, facing the revelling cowboys. One man was out of place amongst the rowdies. He sat alone at the table farthest from the door, a half-full mug of beer in front of him. The handle of a huge Bowie knife protruded above the table, and he wore hard-soled Apache moccasins. Next to the man, a Winchester '73 leaned against the wall. He wore no sidearm.

Randall Johnson drifted up the bar, serving carousers as he came.

The man watched Stryker from under his bleached floppy hat.

'What'll it be, Matt?'

'Two beers.'

'Two?'

Stryker nodded.

Johnson drew the beers. Stryker dug into a vest pocket for a dime and put it on the bar. 'Thanks, Randy. Who's the 'breed at the far table?'

'Dunno. Can't be choosy, though, nowadays. Whomsoever can pay can drink, that's my policy.'

Stryker picked up the beer mugs with his left hand. He kept the sawed-off in the crook of his right arm. He made his way to the rear table, dodging revellers as he went. He stopped at the table. 'Buy you a beer?'

The man looked up. His face was open and honest. Dark eyebrows emphasized the blackness of his eyes. His face bore

17

a color darker than the one that came from being outdoors day after day. 'One beer's 'bout all I drink at one set, Marshal, but you're welcome to buy. Sit?'

Stryker hadn't expected to be asked to sit down, but he showed no surprise. He sat in the chair to the man's left and pushed one of the beers over in front of him.

'I'm Matt Stryker,' he said. 'Marshal of Rimrock, at the moment anyway.'

'Falan Wilder,' the man said. 'Sergeant of Apache scouts at Camp Verde.'

'You the one they call Wolf?'

The man grinned. 'That's what Falan means in Irish talk, and that's what my Cheyenne name means. So, to answer your question, yes.'

Stryker nodded. He leaned the shotgun against the wall next to the Winchester. 'That the rifle you used to shoot all those Apaches?'

'It is. Not that I wanted to kill Apaches.'

'You good with that Bowie?'

Wilder gave Stryker a flat look. He didn't answer.

'OK,' Stryker said, 'I've got reasons for asking. Don't take it personal.'

'I'm not taking it anyway atall, Marshal, but why ask?'

Stryker sipped at his beer. It tasted sour. 'Someone killed a friend of mine tonight,' he said. 'Cut his throat all the way to the backbone. Killer knew how to use a knife and I don't know you, except by reputation. Had to ask.'

Wilder took a swallow of his beer. 'Throat cut, eh?'

'That's how it was.'

'Funny. Most people in this country use guns.'

'My thought, too.'

'Don't want to barge in on your territory, Marshal, but would I be outta line if I asked to see your dead friend? I know a bit about knife cuts and what makes them.'

Stryker took a deep breath. 'Follow me,' he said and stood up, leaving the mug of beer on the table.

Wilder, too, left his beers as they were, taking no farewell sip as he picked up his '73 Winchester.

The crowd of cowboys now stood in a ring around two who glared at each other with doubled fists and stubborn out-thrust chins. Stryker waded through the jeering men. He stepped between the belligerents.

'What's up?' he asked.

'Mel Green here said Bar B cows was all scraggly beasts not fit for a decent dinner table,' the smaller one said. 'Cain't let nobody say things like that about our cows.'

'They ain't your cows, asshole. They belong to Turnhill, and he ain't even American. Shut your filthy trap or I'll knock every one of your teeth straight down your scraggly throat.'

'Have at 'im, Vin. Bust the bastard.' Catcalls came from the rowdy bunch surrounding the would-be fighters.

Stryker shifted the shotgun to his left hand. 'Listen,' he said. 'Quit hollering and listen.'

The cowboys shut up. More than one of them had spent the night in the Rimrock hoosegow, and they knew Stryker didn't make idle conversation.

'Mel. Vin. Every cow on every range around Rimrock is poor this year. It's been dry and feed and water're scarce. Be glad they are still standing. Much more of this weather and you'll all be riding the grub line, y'hear?'

'I still don't like his goldam tone of voice,' Mell said, blustering.

'I don't like the look on your goldam face,' Vin shouted.

'Hold this,' Stryker said, and handed the shotgun to Wilder. He stood nearly six inches taller than either of the cowmen, and half again as broad. He took each by the scruff of his neck and slammed their heads together.

'Shee-it, Marshal. Don't have to break a man's head.' Now Vin whined. Mel just held his head with both hands.

'You two line up at the bar and let Randy give you a drink. No more fighting. Hear?'

'Free?'

'On me,' Stryker said.

'Come on, Mel. Free drinks.'

'Drink,' Stryker said. 'One drink. I'll be back directly to check on you two, so keep the peace. You hear?'

'Hear you, Marshal.' The two men moved to the bar and stood side by side as Johnson poured them each a shot of house whiskey.

'Let's go.' Stryker held his hand out for the shotgun.'

Wilder handed it to him. 'You've got a way with words, Marshal,' he said.

'Matt,' Stryker said. 'Call me Matt.'

'Can we go see that dead man, Matt?'

Stryker motioned toward the door and led Wilder through it into the dark and silent main street of Rimrock.

The lamp in the hotel lobby had burned low, so Stryker gave it a little more wick. He picked it up to light the way to Ruggart's Lucky Seven room. Nothing had changed.

'Can we make that lamp a bit brighter, Matt?'

Stryker ratcheted the lamp wick up until it started smoking, then turned it back until the smoke disappeared. 'That's as bright as the damn thing will go,' he said, 'but it's no great shakes.'

Wilder leaned his Winchester against the wall. 'I'll take a closer look,' he said. He held out his hand for the lamp, and Stryker gave it to him.

He took his time. After a bit he passed the lamp back to Stryker. 'The cut looks big and wide right now, Matt, but that don't mean it was made with a big knife.'

'What was it, you figure?'

'Something uncommon sharp. Straight razor, maybe. One of them knives docs use. Who knows?'

'Surgeon's knife?' Stryker's brow furrowed.

'No sign of any kind of a fight,' Wilder said. 'It's kinda like the dead man just lay down, stuck his neck out, and let it happen.' He held the lamp high and looked around.

'No blood on the floor. Not even a drop. Clean job.' Wilder frowned. 'Sheesh,' he said.

'Clean. Surgical knife,' Stryker said. 'Like it was all planned out.' For the first time, he touched the body. Rigor mortis had set in, and moving Ruggart took some effort. He searched every pocket, and found a billfold with bank drafts in it, a coin purse with three double eagles, an eagle, half a dozen silver dollars, and some small change. A daguerreotype of a little girl with curly blond hair came from a breast pocket. No robbery.

'See anything?' Stryker asked.

'Funny,' Wilder said.

'What's funny?'

'Man with his throat cut, you'd expect a lot of blood,' Wilder said. 'Some here on the bed, but not enough to say a living man had his throat chopped open.' He paused for a moment. 'Ask me, I'd say he was dead before the slicing.'

'Stan's got everything. Don't look like a robbery.'

'Cain't help you any more'n I have,' Wilder said.

'Yeah. Thanks, Wolf . . . Wolf is OK, isn't it?'

'You're Matt. I'm Wolf.'

'Got a place to stay the night?'

'Livery stable.'

Stryker nodded. 'Mind coming by my office before you leave?'

'Sure thing.'

'I'll get Stan buried and such,' Stryker said.

'How long you staying on, Matt?'

21

'Staying on?'

'Rimrock's dead. Folks may stick around for a while, but the town's dead.'

'Yeah.' Wilder said no more.

Stryker closed the door carefully as they left. No robbery. No struggle. No reason a man should die. It was a long walk back to the marshal's office and a long wait for dawn.

3

Stryker awoke with the dawn after spending another night sleeping with his feet up on the marshal's desk. His eyes felt gritty and his face felt like sandpaper to his hand. In most any town, a man could go to the barber for a shave. Not in Rimrock. The barber had pulled out a day or two before, so cutting whiskers was something every man had to do on his own. Stryker decided to wait.

Day comes of a sudden in the high clear air of the Colorado Plateau. One minute the sky in the east grows lighter, the next minute the sun jumps up over the horizon and the world lights up. The only difference is the length of the shadows. With the coming of daylight, Stryker opened the middle drawer of his desk and took out the envelope Stan Ruggart had given him.

Hello, Matt,
You're reading this, so I must be dead. You'll find, when you read my will, that I've made you executor.

This is not something I ask lightly, nor would I ask you if I were unaware that Rimrock will soon be unable to pay for your services. I suggest you quit before the town council (does it still exist?) lets you go.

In the envelope, you will find a bank draft for $500

made out to you. I would like to think the money will buy two months of your time.

What, you might ask, will cost two months of your valuable time?

I have a daughter, Matt. I've not seen her since she was a button, but she's my only kin. I have no idea where her mother is or if she has any interest in April's welfare. An aside: in happier days, we were going to name our baby May if it was a girl and Martin if a boy. But she came early. Her birthday fell in April, so that's what we named her.

One more thing. April's mother Elizabeth, also known as Lizzimae, could possibly come out of the woodwork, seeking a share of what's in my will. I've provided for a one-time payout. And for her, that's it.

Matt, although I own a 25% share of the Dominion mine in Mother Lode, that is not where my money is. Part of it is in Denver, put to work by Josiah Fish buying cattle, hogs, corn, wheat, or anything else necessary to feed all the people who are and will be coming West. Part of it is in San Francisco, where Levi Gries, an honest man, uses the income to help April. And part of it is in gold, this also handled by Josiah Fish.

The payments from the mine go into an account in Prescott. The $500 draft is on Wells Fargo there.

Matt, please find the person who killed me. I have no idea who it was, though I have felt threats from several quarters. Whoever did me in needs to face the consequences (I hate to say justice), and I know of no better man to do the job. Consider it a final favor to the town drunk.

And thank you, Matt. Thank you.

One more thing. If Lizzimae comes looking for a handout, give her what is in the Prescott Wells Fargo account, otherwise follow my will. I trust you to create a new account, wherever you see fit, to accept the mine income. Talk it over with Josiah. Again, thank you, my friend, thank you.

Stryker folded the letter and put it back in the envelope next to the sealed Last Will and Testament of Stanford Jameson Ruggart. He opened the bottom right-hand drawer and put the envelope beneath a pile of Wanted fliers. Then he pulled it out again. It needed to go somewhere safe, and at the moment, he had no idea where 'safe' might be.

In the end, he got his saddle-bags, undid the lacing on the two layers of leather between the bags, slipped the envelope inside, and redid the lacing. He dropped the empty saddle-bags on the floor as if by afterthought. No one in Rimrock would steal an empty pair of saddle-bags.

The town began to stir as Stryker left his office and strode down Washington Way toward the sign that read FOOD. Halfway to the eatery, he changed directions and went to the livery.

'Rube,' he called. 'Oh, Rube.'

Ruben Wilcox came from the direction of the back stalls, a broad-shouldered man who smelled of the horses he tended.

'Ruben, Marshal. How many times do I gotta tell you to call me Ruben? No man likes to be called a rube.'

'Sorry,' Stryker said, as always, 'Rube.'

'Goldammit, Marshal. Ruben.'

'Right. Ruben. Stan Ruggart is dead, lying in room seven at the hotel.'

'Jeez. Who done it?'

'Wish I knew. Could you do a couple of things for me?'

'Sure.'

'I don't imagine there's lumber around for a pine box, so

25

could you stitch together a canvas bag to bury Stan in?'

'Reckon I could do that.'

'And could you get someone to help you dig a grave? Five dollars each for the digging.'

Wilcox's eyes lit up when he heard five dollars. 'No problem, Marshal,' he said. 'Wonder who done it, though.'

'Tell me. You seen any strangers around lately?'

'Don't see much of anybody lately, Marshal. When you leaving?'

Stryker gave Wilcox a sharp look. 'Who said I was leaving?'

'Hell, Marshal, everybody's leaving. It's just a matter of when,' Wilcox said with a rueful smile. 'I mean, I seen the barber leaving yesterday and I reckon I'll fold up afore long. I'll get Ruggart's bag ready. Grave should be ready by noon or so. The ground's hard as rock in that graveyard.'

' 'Preciate it, Rube . . . en.'

Wilcox waved a hand and went back into the dark of the big barn. Stryker again strode toward Charlie Stark's place.

'Beef and beans, Marshal,' Charlie called from the kitchen as Stryker entered.

'Fine,' Stryker said.

Stark's FOOD place had six tables and two customers. One was Tom Hall, the other Wolf Wilder. They ignored each other.

By habit, Stryker sat at the same table as always, his back to the wall. 'Tom. Wolf. You two want to join me?'

The men exchanged glances and little smiles of mutual respect.

'Thank you, Matt,' Wilder said. He picked up his coffee mug and moved to the chair at Stryker's right. Hall sat on his left.

'Wolf Wilder, eh? I heard about that Apache fight. Musta been some tough going there for a while,' Hall said.

'Good morning to you, too, Thomas Hall,' Wilder said.

'We'll bury Stan at noon,' Stryker said.

Charlie Stark brought three plates of beef boiled with beans. 'Be back with coffee shortly,' he said. 'Sourdough or salcratus?'

'Sourdough,' Stryker said.

'Same,' said the other two.

'We'll talk after we eat,' Stryker said. He dug into the beef and beans. Damn, but Charlie Stark was a good cook. Something as basic as beef and beans tasted like it should be served in the Bon Apetit or whatever that Frenchy restaurant in Prescott was called. Stryker savored the breakfast, looking up briefly when Stark came with coffee and bread.

'You sucked down that grub like you ain't had nothing to eat for a month of Sundays, Matt.' Wilder took a gulp of his coffee.

'Reckon I kinda forgot about eating yesterday,' Stryker said. 'Not like there's a store on every corner, open all hours. I've been hungry before and I'll be hungry again.'

'Where's it going from here, Marshal?' Hall's question came in a flat matter-of-fact voice. 'Got a plan?'

Stryker took a deep breath. 'Sort of,' he said. He glanced at Wilder.

'Wolf, I know you've got to get back to Camp Verde, but could you take an hour or two and see what sign you can find in the dead man's room? You've got eyes that can see a lot more than mine. That possible?'

'You buying breakfast?' Wilder showed his ghost of a smile.

'That's the least I can do,' Stryker said.

'Deal.'

Stryker turned to Tom Hall. 'You said someone hired you to protect Stan Ruggart.'

Hall gave Stryker a long look. 'That's right,' he said.

'Not saying who?'

'Can't. Gave my word.'

This time Stryker gave Hall a long look. The silence stretched. 'Stan's dead,' he said, at last.

'We gonna catch who done it?'

'I reckon.'

'Then let's get to catching,' Hall said.

'We'll not move until Stan's buried,' Stryker said. 'And we'll listen to what Wolf Wilder has to say before we do anything.'

'You're the marshal,' Hall said. 'I just want to be there when the doer gets tagged.'

'Why you taking this so personal?'

'I took money to protect a man. He's dead. Seems to me I should get that killer. Matter of professional concern.'

'I'll be going over to the cadaver's room,' Wilder said. 'Give me an hour or so. If there's anything of interest in that room, I'll find it.'

'Look me up when you've finished. I'll be in the office or in the President, if you don't see me on the street.'

'OK, Matt,' Wilder said. He scraped his chair back, reached for his Winchester, and stood. The rifle fit naturally in the crook of his left arm, carried Indian fashion, muzzle high, action to hand. With a glance around the room, he left, quietly closing the door behind him.

'So that's Wolf Wilder?' Hall said. 'They say he held off a couple dozen Apaches after they'd shot his lieutenant down.'

'That's what they say. I reckon they don't call him "Wolf" for nothing.' Stryker pinned Hall with a hard look. 'I'm not going to ask you who hired Stan's protection again, Tom. But if you're holding back something that might tell us who the killer is . . .' He let the statement hang.

Hall said nothing.

28

'All right. We'll give the wolf a couple of hours to nose around. Then we'll leave for Prescott. While we're waiting, you do whatever you can think of to raise killer sign. I'll go resign as marshal of Rimrock.' Stryker stood. 'I'll see you in the President later,' he said.

A town council of five men had hired Matt Stryker but only two of them were still in town: Randall Johnson of the President saloon and Bartholomew Goldfinch, who owned the town's only general store. If it weren't for the Rocking R, the Lazy B Cross, and the Flying M, Goldfinch would have been long gone. As it was, he owned the only business in town that didn't look on its last legs.

Matt Stryker walked into Rimrock general store moments after Goldfinch opened for business.

'Be with you in a minute, Marshal,' Goldfinch called from the back room.

Stryker stood by the Ritty cash register, a new-fangled machine that Goldfinch had brought in when Rimrock mines operated full blast and the town rocked on its foundation as men, machines, and draft animals gouged silver and gold from grudging lode stone to pay for their excesses.

'What'll it be, Matt?' Goldfinch came from the back, wiping his slim white hands on the canvas apron he habitually wore.

Stryker unpinned the badge from his vest and put it on the counter. 'Came to resign, Bart. Town has no more need of me. Besides, you can't afford a marshal. You can hardly afford to be a town.'

Goldfinch frowned. 'Don't like you doing this, Matt. Really don't.'

Stryker said nothing. Then, 'I'll be pulling out this afternoon, Bart. Town owes me for a month and a half, but I'd settle for an even month's pay. Reckon you can scrape that much together?'

Goldfinch looked like he'd eaten a sour plum.

'A hundred's too much, then?'

Goldfinch cleared his throat. 'Well, Matt. If you're bound and determined to leave our town lawless. . . .'

'I'm leaving, Bart. I'll come back by the store this afternoon to collect my back pay.' Stryker turned and strode from the store. He couldn't help noticing that many of the shelves were bare.

Back in his office, Stryker began cleaning out the desk, separating items to be left from those to throw on the refuse heap. Old receipts, chits, notes on people to watch for, tally sheets, records of meals served, warrants filled . . . the list seemed endless. Still, Stryker stolidly culled the useless from the useful, piling one on the right, the other on the left.

'Marshal?'

Stryker looked up.

'Ready to plant Ruggart, Marshal. He fits in that canvas bag I made,' Ruben Wilcox said. 'Starting to stink, though.'

'Got a wagon to haul him in?'

'Sitting out front of the hotel right this here minute, Marshal.'

'Thanks, Rube . . . er, Ruben. I'll be right along. You and your helper get Stan loaded, OK?'

Wilcox held out his hand.

Stryker arched an eyebrow.

'Five bucks for me and five for Wilbur Banks,' Wilcox said.

'Shit,' Stryker said. 'The man ain't even planted yet.'

'Heard for sure you was leaving, Marshal. Want the fivers you promised afore you get aboard that there Araby stud horse and skedaddle.'

Stryker barked a little laugh. 'That's right. I'm outta here, Ruben.' He dug an eagle from his pocket and handed it to Wilcox. 'You'll have to settle with Wilbur,' he said.

'Knew you was a man of his word, Marshal, but a feller can't be too careful, you know. No offense meant.'

'None taken. Get Stan loaded. I'll be there directly.'

Wilcox left, a big smile on his face. Stryker stepped to the door to watch him, and saw him disappearing through the batwing doors of the President. *Fortifying himself against the smell.* Stryker returned to the desk.

Paperwork lay in two piles, one for filing, one for the trash. Stryker dug the Wanted fliers from the bottom drawer. He'd been meaning to go through them for weeks, but never seemed to get around to it. Some other more important task could always be made up instead.

Stryker smiled at some of the names outlaws were given, or in some cases, took for themselves. Black Bart. Silver Fox. Kid Swingle. Johnny behind the Deuce. Ma Dillon. Barber Orv.

Barber Orvil Randall. Still at large. Five foot seven inches in height. Slight of build. Very light-blue eyes. Light-brown hair. Clean shaven. Tends to dandy dress. Small scar over left eye. Sometimes works as a doctor. The drawing showed a boyish face, eyes drooping at the outer corners. And, at the bottom of the description *cuts victims post-mortem, leaving the appearance of lethal wounds, but lack of bleeding from the wounds indicate they were inflicted after death. The wounds, seemingly from a straight razor, earned Orvil Randall his barber epithet. Nevertheless, Randall is an accomplished barber and sometime doctor. He only kills for hire.*

4

Six men buried Stan Ruggart: Ruben Wilcox, Wilbur Banks, Randy Johnson, Wolf Wilder, Tom Hall, and Matt Stryker. No words over the grave. No eulogy. They lowered the body in its canvas bag with two lariats from the livery stable, and covered it with the hard clods that Wilcox and Banks had hacked from the dry earth with crowbars and pickaxes.

Matt shoved a headboard into the edge of the grave. He'd burned Ruggart's epitaph into the old board with a running iron borrowed from Wilcox.

Stanford Jameson Ruggart
A good man who loved good whiskey
Murdered
May 27, 1879

'Thanks, Ruben, Wilbur,' Stryker said.
'Not a pretty way to die,' Wilcox said.
'There is no pretty way.' Stryker turned and started down the hill toward Rimrock. Wilder and Hall followed him in silence. Randy rode in the wagon with Wilcox and Banks.
'Talk back at the office?' Stryker said.
'Still use it?' Hall asked.
'I reckon. No one else wears the star,' said Stryker.

'Got coffee?' Wilder matched Stryker stride for stride. Hall lagged half a step behind.

'I'll get some. You all wait here.' Stryker left Wilder and Hall at the marshal's office while he went to Charlie Stark's place for a pot of coffee. When he returned, the two men sat on opposite sides of the room. Hall had his chair tipped against the wall, his hat pulled down over his eyes.

'Am I interrupting something important?' Stryker put cups on the desk and filled them with coffee. Neither Wilder nor Hall said anything. Stryker handed them cups of hot coffee.

A wagon rattled by, the first one on Washington Way since the one carrying Ruggart's remains had gone to the cemetery.

Stryker took a sip of coffee. He savored the strong brew before swallowing. 'Find anything worth talking about?' he asked Wilder.

Wilder shook his head. 'Nothing. The room was like someone had already done the Saturday cleaning. Never seen a place so spick and span.'

'Shit.'

'Yeah.'

'So now what?' Hall said.

'Stan wants me to find his killer, and do some other things. I reckon if I go on doing those other things, them who wanted him dead will want me dead, too, but when they come after me, I won't just roll over and die.'

'I gotta be moving on,' Wilder said. 'Need to get to Camp Verde.'

'Thanks, Wolf.'

'Sorry I weren't no help.'

Stryker stood and held out his hand. 'Mighty pleased to make your acquaintance, Wolf Wilder,' he said.

Wilder took the proffered hand. 'My pleasure, Matt

Stryker. Perhaps we'll get together again down the trail.'

Stryker smiled. 'We can hope,' he said.

Wilder paused a moment just inside the door, inspecting near-empty Washington Way. He stepped outside, moving to the left and putting his back against the building. After a moment he walked away, moving diagonally across the street toward the livery.

'Careful man,' Hall said.

'He is. He'll outlive us both.'

A fly buzzed in the silence, trying to escape through the glass of the windowpane to the bright day outside.

'Well?'

'Well what?' Stryker said.

'Well, what're you gonna do now?'

'Go to Prescott.'

'That's it?'

'That's it.'

'Shee-it. Goldam varmit-hunting Matt Stryker here with a man not an hour buried and tells me he's going to gawd-awful Prescott. I don't see no killer trails pointing at Prescott.'

'You don't have to tag along. Fact, I'd probably do better on my own.'

Hall sat back in his chair. He glared at Stryker. Then smiled. 'Hell. I don't know my ass from a hole in the ground, Matt Stryker. You don't mind, I'll tag along. May learn something. May not. But I can't help thinking things will get interesting.' He stood and arranged his Stetson square on his square-jawed head. 'I'll be at the President,' he said, 'pick me up when you leave.'

Stryker took the trash out back and threw it on the rubbish pile. Back inside, he buckled on his six-gun, retrieved his Winchester from the gun rack, stuffed two boxes of .44-40 cartridges into the offside saddle-bag, tossed his keys on to the desk, and left the Rimrock marshal's office for the last time.

Shouldering the saddle-bags, Stryker walked down Washington Way toward the hotel. He'd lived in Rimrock a few months over two years, and the town was now a mere ghost of its boomtown days.

He stopped in the empty lobby. Someone had crossed Stan Ruggart's name off the registry book. Stryker took his own key from the rack. No. 13. Unlucky thirteen? He'd never given the myth any thought. He couldn't even remember why he'd chosen thirteen. Maybe it had been the only room available back then. He climbed the stairs, walked down the hall . . . and stopped. Wolf Wilder had not assumed the streets of Rimrock were safe. He'd not assume his room was safe.

Stryker set the saddle-bags by the wall without making a sound. He leaned the Winchester against the same wall. He drew his Remington Army and cocked it, stood as far to the left of the door as he could, squatted, inserted the key . . . and waited.

Nothing.

He turned the key.

A shotgun blast tore through the door, taking out the knob and lock assembly and smashing a foot-wide hole in the panelling.

Stryker answered the blast with four shots from his Remington, evenly spaced across the door, matching the angle of the shotgun blast.

No return shots.

He ejected the spent cartridges and fed five new ones into the Remington's cylinder.

A rustle and a thump came from inside the room. Stryker smashed a shoulder into the door, separating the top from the bottom. He hit the floor with his left shoulder down and rolled quickly past the end of the bed. A boot protruded from the other side.

Remington cocked, Stryker got to his knees.

The boot didn't move.

He stood.

The boot didn't move.

He jostled it with his own boot. It flopped back and forth. Pistol ready, Stryker stepped around the end of the bed. A man lay crumpled in the space between the bed and the wall. A shotgun lay half on the floor, half across his chest. A trickle of blood had run from the bullet hole in the center of his forehead. *Couldn't have shot that straight by aiming.* Blood pooled beneath his head, showing there was an exit wound. The man's pale yellow eyes were open and his mouth stretched in a soundless scream. He had no tongue.

Dumb Dickie.

Stryker had heard of the assassin with no tongue but had never crossed paths with him. *Funny he could get into town without me seeing him.*

Feet pounded up the stairs. Stryker stepped to the broken door, gun in hand.

'Matt?'

'I'm OK.'

'Damn. Who's shooting at people now?'

'Dumb Dickie.'

Hall looked in. 'No shit? Dumb Dickie?'

'You know him?'

'Reputation. Maybe we'd better have a look at what's in his pockets.'

Stryker took another look at Hall. 'Sure you ain't a lawman?'

'I have been. Just like you.'

'Range detective pays better, then?'

'Sometimes. I'm not comfortable staying in the same town too long.'

'That bad?'

'It wasn't fun and she didn't make it out.'

Stryker frowned at the familiar story. 'Let's have a look at Dickie. Wonder who he was killing for ... and why me?' Stryker's innards still twitched from considering what the shotgun pellets would have done to them. He bent down to straighten Dumb Dickie's leg. 'New boots,' he said. 'Not enough wear to notice.'

He grabbed Dickie's ankles and dragged him out on to the threadbare rug. 'New clothes, too. Ain't dusty like they'd be from a long ride. We'll need to ask Goldfinch who he sold clothes to.'

'Sheesh. You couldn't a hit him more dead center if you'd been shooting from two inches.'

'Dead luck. I shot through the door. Couldn't see a thing.'

Dumb Dickie wore a wool coat over a leather vest and gray California pants. His new boots were low-heel of a style called wellington. They had little dust on them. Strange. Stryker unbuttoned the coat and checked the inside pockets. Nothing.

The vest pockets held nothing either, but in Dumb Dickie's shirt pocket Stryker found a sack of Bull Durham and a packet of cigarette papers, which he handed to Hall. 'Damn. Nothing useful,' he said, and rolled Dickie over to search his hip pockets.

'Hey!'

'What?' Stryker worked at getting Dickie face up again.

'Wouldja have a gander at this.' Hall held the packet of papers in one hand and a tightly folded piece of paper in the other. He stuffed the cigarette papers in his vest pocket and started to open the folded one.

'Hold it. Let me have a look before you open it.'

Hall handed the folded paper to Stryker. 'You're the one

37

he shot at,' he said.

Stryker unfolded the paper, a page torn from something small, a tally book, perhaps. The message, printed in block letters, read:

MATTHEW STRYKER
RIMROCK, ARIZONA
$500

He turned the page so Hall could read it.

'Shee-it. You're worth money, man. You better watch your back, or let me. Whoever bought Dumb Dickie's sure to buy more gunnies, or other kinds of killers.'

'Why should you watch my back?' Stryker said as he continued his search of the dead man's clothing.

'Well, I was paid a fair amount to look after Stan Ruggart. Wasn't able to fill that contract,' Hall said. 'But I figure watching your back might do to fill part of it. I reckon Ruggart would want me to do that.'

Stryker shot a glance at Tom Hall's deadpan face. 'OK,' he said. 'You're on.' With Dickie face up, he started on the front pants pockets.

'Nothing else?'

'Doesn't seem to be,' Stryker said, 'but I'll have a look at those new boots.'

'Man's not wearing a gun,' Hall said. 'Wonder if that's usual for him.'

Stryker shrugged. He patted the assassin's hips where a gun rig would be fastened. 'New clothes don't show the wear of a gun rig.' His hand stopped a little above the pants' waist. 'Dickie's got some kind of rig on,' he said. He undid the buttons of Dickie's shirt, unbuckled a money belt, and pulled it from the body.

'Two of the pockets got nothing in them,' Stryker said

after patting the money belt. He dug six double eagles from each of the other two pockets. 'Two hundred forty. I reckon he got half the five hundred on me in advance.'

Hall held out a hand. 'Lemme see.'

Stryker gave him a double eagle.

Hall turned the coin over several times, then bit on it. 'Brand new,' he said. 'Gold, too. Bites right.'

'So? I can see that.'

'So how many spankin' new twenty-dollar gold pieces have you seen?'

'A few.'

'Where at?'

Stryker knew Hall was leading him, but he played along. 'Wells Fargo. National Bank of Denver. Got paid by the army once with brand new coins. Just once.'

'Army?'

'Yeah. CSA.'

Hall chuckled. 'Can't figure Rebs with new gold.'

'We took it from Yanks. Hit a train just outta Chattanooga about a month before Appomattox. The colonel decided it was better we got paid, back pay and all, than try to get the coins across the mountains to Richmond.'

'Smart colonel. Anyone I know?'

Stryker gave Hall a piercing glance. 'Could be,' he said.

Hall chuckled again. 'I reckon,' he said.

Stryker added five double eagles to the one in Hall's hand. 'Dickie's got no use for those,' he said. 'Should keep you in line grub while we're on the trail. Let's go down to Prescott. That OK with you?'

Hall closed his long fingers around the gold coins. 'You lead off, Matthew Stryker. I'll ride along to cover your back.'

Stryker gave him a long look. 'Counting on that, Tom Hall. Now. Let's get out of here.'

The two men left Dumb Dickie's body lying in the hotel

room. Stryker picked up his rifle and saddle-bags, and they strode from the lobby side by side, one tall and dark and dressed in black, the other blond, a bit shorter, slim, and dressed in tan pants, off-white shirt, and brown leather vest. Stryker's Remington rode comfortably in a right-hand tie-down holster. Hall's six-gun hung aslant, high on his left hip, handle ready for an easy cross-draw with his right hand. People naturally stepped out of their way as the men catty-cornered across Washington Way toward Rimrock general store.

One wagon crept up Washington Way as if ashamed to be the only thing moving when the rest of the town was so silent. It pulled up in front of the store as Stryker and Hall mounted the steps to the porch and went into Goldfinch's store.

'Bart!'

'Be right there.'

The storekeeper came from the back room, wiping his hands on the apron he habitually wore. 'What'll it be, Matt?'

'Dead man in my room at the hotel, Bart. I've got what I need from the room, so I'd appreciate you getting someone to plant the body.'

'Another one?'

'Yep. Dumb Dickie Evans. Didn't you hear the shotgun blast?'

'Didn't notice.'

'Don't look like anyone did. Don't matter one way or the other. One question, though. Dumb Dickie was wearing brand-new store-bought duds. Wondered if he got 'em here, and if anybody was with him.'

'No grown men,' Goldfinch said. 'But there was a young feller in here yesterday. He bought clothes and boots. Said they was for his pa.'

Damn. Stryker looked at Tom Hall. 'Never paid no mind

to any kids,' he said. 'You notice any?'

Hall shook his head. 'What've we got on the street at any one time? Maybe twenty people. Makes a man go to sleep. Gets so you don't look at anybody because you'd always see the same people.'

Stryker nodded. 'Puts many to sleep all right. But it was my job to notice. Man. Woman. Child. I'm supposed to know what's going on.'

He paused a moment, chin on his chest, thinking. He took a deep breath. 'Don't matter much, I reckon,' he said. 'Let's go to Prescott. That'll shake some apples out of the tree.'

'You might want to think about sticking around, Marshal,' Goldfinch said. 'The Daggs brothers are bringing in fifty thousand sheep and they say the railway's gonna come across the top of the rim all the way to San Fran. Change for the good, I'd say. Rimrock ain't dead yet.'

5

'The vein's getting thin, Mr McKendrick,' Axel Swain said. 'Silver content is down to fifty ounces a ton. If it keeps on like this, we'll be paying out of pocket to dig Dominion ore.'

'You don't see the situation improving, then?' Rod McKendrick frowned and ran a hand through his mane of reddish hair.

'No, sir. Were it me, I'd cut and run while there's still a bit of silver left.'

'Thank you, Axel. Excellent information, as always.'

'Do we keep digging?'

'For the moment. For the moment.'

'Yes, sir.' Swain stood to leave.

'Keep this to yourself, Axel,' McKendrick said.

'Yes, sir.' Swain clapped a cloth cap on his head, knuckled his forehead in salute, and left the office, trailing the scent of old cigars.

McKendrick turned in his swivel chair, laced his fingers behind a thick neck, and stared out the window at bustling Glory Road, the main street of the mining town everyone called Mother Lode.

He cursed his luck. Dominion had been putting out a solid sixty ounces a ton when he bought the mine from Stanford Ruggart and Milford Flake back in '75. True,

Ruggart kept a quarter share in the enterprise, but promised to stay out of day-to-day operations. McKendrick paid Ruggart twenty-five per cent of Consolidation Mine's profits every three months. Sent the money, such as it was after all the costs and hints of costs were removed, to a bank in Prescott, Arizona.

McKendrick took out a five-year note from a bank in San Francisco to pay for the mine. The note fell due at the beginning of the year. Best find a buyer for the Dominion, quick.

Two weeks passed and the grade of Dominion ore stayed above fifty ounces to the ton. Then the lower southeast shaft ran dry. The miners hacked solid rock from the shaft for three days, but the spoil showed only the barest trace of silver.

'Keep a shift working that shaft,' McKendrick ordered.

'Yes, sir,' said Swain, 'but there ain't no silver down there.'

'Just keep them working.'

'Yes, sir.'

McKendrick again turned his gaze to the bustle on Glory Road, watching the flood of wagons, men, and some women as he considered the dry shaft. Although Mother Lode's silver was discovered nearly five years ago, the town still felt like a boom camp.

He owned six of the twenty-seven saloons on Glory Road, and one in Sorryton, a cluster of tarpapered shacks and tumbledown adobes where Mexicans and Indians and down-and-out whites struggled for subsistence.

'Williams,' McKendrick barked.

A moment later, 'Shortly, sir. Shortly.'

A rap on the door.

'Come.'

Williams entered, a tall man stooped at the shoulders with a green eyeshade, spectacles, and ink-stained right forefinger and thumb. 'You called, sir.'

McKendrick looked up from the paperwork on his desk. 'Yes, Williams, I did. I need to contact Kensington St George.' He handed a folded sheet of paper to Williams. 'Go over to the telegraph station and see that Sparky sends this message to St George. Have him wire it to Yuma, Prescott, San Francisco, Denver, and Salt Lake City. Oh, add El Paso to that list.'

'Immediately, sir.'

'And send Black Reynolds to see me.'

'Black Reynolds?'

'That's what I said. See if you can get word to him quietly.'

'Yes, sir.' Williams hesitated. 'Are you sure you want him to come here, sir?'

'Why not?'

'Well, sir, Black is not a savory person and people seeing him come in and out of Dominion headquarters may draw the wrong conclusions, sir.'

'Hmmm. You may be right, Williams.'

'Yes, sir. May I be so bold as to point out that you own a controlling interest in the Painted Pony, sir, on Glory Road. Perhaps the saloon's bookkeeping needs to be inspected, sir.'

'Good point. Tell Herb Gallagher I'll visit the Painted Pony tonight. Have Black Reynolds meet me in the saloon's office. It has a back door, if I remember correctly.'

'Yes, sir. Right away, sir. I'll get the telegram off first, sir.'

Most of the twenty-seven saloons on Glory Road were single-storied affairs that served house whiskey out of a barrel. Some were two-storied buildings with girls to keep customers happy, push drinks, and take the occasional big spender upstairs. These houses of nocturnal amusement served house whiskey, of course, but also had several brands of good liquor – Old Potrero, Turley's Mill, Old Overholt, Kessler – as well as beer brewed by Gustaff Sachsenhausen in the German tradition.

But the Painted Pony stood out, rivalled only by Balm of Gilead. Both saloons stood three stories high. The ground floor catered to serious drinkers, the second to serious gamblers, and the third to those who paid for feminine wiles by the hour, or by the night.

It served not only whiskey and beer, but also fine wine. The more expensive vintages came from France and Italy but, for a modest outlay, the more sophisticated of the Painted Pony's drinkers could have surprisingly good wine from the El Aliso winery in Los Angeles, red or white.

Gallagher stood outside the Painted Pony when McKendrick's carriage arrived. 'Good of you to visit us, Mr McKendrick,' he said, his face expressionless.

'Come back in one hour,' McKendrick told the driver. He brushed past Gallagher and entered the saloon. 'Come talk with me,' he said.

'Yes, sir.' Gallagher followed half a step behind as McKendrick made straight for the office door, which stood almost hidden behind the stairs rising to the second floor.

A man in shirtsleeves and suspenders pounded out a clanky version of *Green Grow the Lilacs* on an upright piano. Shrill feminine laughter punctuated the drone of male voices. Glasses clanked as the serious drinkers got on with their business.

'Bring a bottle of El Aliso red,' McKendrick said. 'And a hunk of that cheddar from Arvil Smithson's dairy, if you've got some.'

'Yes, sir.' Gallagher detoured to get McKendrick's order.

McKendrick pushed open the office door without knocking.

'Oh!' A young woman started, and straightened up.

'What're you doing in here?'

The woman looked at McKendrick with a disturbingly

frank gaze. 'I might ask you the same thing, sir. Who are you, and what gives you the right to barge into this office without so much as a "by your leave"?'

'The question stands.'

'Yes, it does. My question.'

The tall woman's dark brown hair was pulled into a no-nonsense bun at the nape of her neck, and her makeup was lightly and skilfully applied. While she wasn't a matron from Lincoln Heights, she also was not a run-of-the-mill whore.

'Name's Rodham McKendrick. I own the lion's share of this saloon.'

'And my name is Catherine de Merode. I am in charge of floor services here.'

'That still doesn't tell me why the hell you're in this office,' McKendrick said.

'My dear Mr Kendrick. A woman sometimes must make adjustments to her clothing that she'd rather not make in front of every drunken miner or teamster east of San Francisco. That is why I'm in your holy office. I can certainly be more specific about what I was doing if you are unable to draw a simple conclusion from what I have said. Sir.'

McKendrick stood stock still, his lips open slightly. Catherine, for some reason, he thought of her as Catherine, now had sparks of fire in her eyes and her cheeks flushed with anger. Her beauty went far beyond any he'd ever seen.

'Are you tongue-tied, then, Mr McKendrick?' Catherine asked. 'Need I slap your face to get your attention, then?'

A slow smile came to McKendrick's face. 'Oh, no, ma'am. Thank you for your explanation. It was abundantly clear. And I beg your pardon for barging in at a delicate moment.'

A fleeting look of satisfaction crossed Catherine's face.

'Now, if you could please vacate the office. I'm expecting a visitor, and Mr Gallagher and I have business to discuss. If you please.' McKendrick made a little bow and indicated the door with an outstretched hand.

Catherine glared at him. 'If you were slightly more civil,' she said, 'you might be a handsome man. Good evening, Mr McKendrick.' She lifted her skirts and sailed through the door. McKendrick heard her melodious laugh as she moved across the saloon. He shook his head and sat in the big chair behind the desk. Maybe a cheroot would clear his mind.

Gallagher brought the wine and cheese just as McKendrick got the cheroot well lit. He uncorked the bottle, poured a bit into a stem glass, and held it out.

McKendrick took the glass, cupped it in his palm to warm it slightly, savored the deep, nutty aroma, and sipped at the dark purple wine. He smiled. 'First rate. Very good.'

Gallagher smiled as well. 'We've had this bottle in the cellar for almost five years, sir.'

'Cellar?' McKendrick was not a wine drinker by habit.

'Oh, yes. When you told me to stock wine, sir, I had a cellar dug. Wine always tastes better when slightly cool. The cellar keeps it just right.'

'Very well.'

'Thank you, sir.'

'And how is business?'

Gallagher frowned. 'Glory Road's not quite what it was. People are saying the silver may be playing out. The Silver King and Medusa mines have let some of their miners go. The men who come here don't seem to have as much money to spend.'

McKendrick nodded. 'Thought as much,' he said. 'Thank you, Gallagher. I'd like to use the office for an hour or so. Please post someone to see that I'm not disturbed.'

Gallagher stood for a moment but McKendrick ignored him. He made a little bow and went back into the saloon. McKendrick drew deeply on his cheroot and settled back to wait for Black Reynolds.

The knock came when the cheroot was a nub. McKendrick tossed it into a brass spittoon. 'Come,' he said.

Williams stuck his head in the back door. 'All clear, sir?'

'Bring him in.'

'Yes, sir.' Williams disappeared and a small man in dirty overalls and run-over shoes entered the room. He snatched a greasy cloth cap from his head. 'G'day, guv,' he said. 'Yur man say you want a word. Well, guv, here I is.'

McKendrick leaned forward, pinning the little man with a piercing gaze. 'You're Black Reynolds, then. I've heard much about you.'

'I yam, guv.'

'I hear you work magic with a stick of dynamite,' McKendrick said.

'It no be magic, guv. But the blow always do what I tells it to.'

'Then I have a job of magic for your dynamite sticks,' McKendrik said, 'and it pays a full hundred dollars.'

Black Reynolds squinted at McKendrick. 'A hundred, eh? Well, just so's you know, I'll not kill anyone with my sticks. I'll move earth and rocks, guv, or knock down yur building, if that's what you wants. But I dunna kill.'

McKendrick laughed. 'I'm not looking for dead bodies, man.'

'A hunnert be lots of boodle, guv.'

'I want you to seal the lower southeast shaft in the Dominion mine,' McKendrick said. 'And make it look like something happened naturally. Can you work that kind of magic?'

Black Reynolds squinted at McKendrick again. 'Got sumpin down there you don't want folks to know about, then? I'm thinking a hunnert ain't quite enough to do the job up proper like.'

McKendrick poured a glass of El Aliso red and set it on

the desk in front of Reynolds. 'Ambrosia,' he said. 'Try it.'

'Say again, guv.'

'Ambrosia.'

Reynolds shook his head. 'Looks like wine to me.' He took the glass, ignoring the stem, and gulped a large swallow. 'Don't carry a kick like good whiskey, but it do tickle the throat right pleasant.' He chugged the rest of the wine. 'A hunnert ain't enough.' He set the glass carefully on the desk and sat staring at McKendrick with an expectant expression on his face.

'What's your idea of a fair price, Black?'

'Dunno. Thousand. Ten thousand. 'S not my idea what counts, it be what my work are worth to you. I'm thinking a hunnert are chicken feed to the hog trough you feed at.'

'You have a way with words.'

Black Reynolds sat perfectly still. He didn't look away like most people would when McKendrick gave him a hard look.

McKendrick had come prepared to pay Black Reynolds in advance. He plucked a small poke from his coat pocket and dropped it on the desk. Its contents chinked softly. 'One hundred dollars in gold eagles,' he said.

Reynolds sat still.

McKendrick heaved himself to his feet, walked to the door, and jerked it open. 'Tell Gallagher to come here,' he said to the man standing guard. He turned to Black Reynolds. 'I'm going to give you an advance of five hundred dollars,' he said. 'Consider that half your fee. When the job is done, you'll get another five hundred. After that, it would be in the interest of your good health to leave Mother Lode. If I see you around, or if I hear of any big spending on your account, I'll have you killed.'

6

'Mr Swain seems anxious to speak with you, sir,' Williams said from the doorway.

'Send him in.'

Swain swiped his cap from his head as he entered. 'Explosion in the southeast shaft, Mr McKendrick.'

'My God. Any miners hurt?'

'Not that I know of, sir. The blast came just after the graveyard shift had come to the lift and before the day shift went into the shaft. Mighty lucky, I'd say, sir. But the shaft is down. No way to dig through that spoil. Well, we could do it, but the job would take a month or so. . . .' Swain's voice trailed off.

McKendrick heaved a sigh. 'Perhaps it's best we don't dig the shaft out right away. Don't say whether we'll reopen it or not. Lay off who you can for whatever reason, and spread the others out through the teams working the remaining shafts.'

'Yes, sir. Ore from the other shafts is still at or above sixty ounces per ton. Dominion will do OK, sir.'

'Yes, yes. But start looking for ways to cut expenses, Axel. We must assume the other shafts will go the way of the southeast one. Maximize profits. Your bonus will be ten per cent of the net at the end of the year.'

Swain's face lit up. 'Yes. Sir! Dominion will do well, I promise.'

McKendrick waved him away. 'Thank you, Axel. I'm depending on you,' he said.

Two days later, Kensington St George arrived in Mother Lode. He rode into town on a dapple gray mare he called Sweetheart. His gray plainsman hat showed the dust of the trail, as did his burgundy frock-coat. A royal-blue sash around his waist carried two Colt Lightning model pistols in .38 caliber. A custom holster hanging from the pommel carried a sawed-off Parker Bros. 10-gauge shotgun with pistol grips and 12-inch barrels. He left Sweetheart at Davidson's livery with instructions to grain her well and curry her twice a day. With saddle-bags over his shoulder and the Parker Bros. in his left hand, St George walked to the Rassiter House on Plum Street, just off Glory Road.

'I'll take your best room,' St George said to the man at the hotel counter.

'Very good, sir.'

'Rod McKendrick will pay,' he said, 'so send up a bottle of Madeira . . . you do have Madeira, don't you?'

'Yes, sir.'

'And find me the best-looking girl in town, if you know what I mean.'

'The hotel does not engage in procurement, sir,' the clerk said.

'Find me someone who does.'

'Sign the register, sir?'

He wrote *Kensington St George* in bold script.

'Your key, sir.'

St George smiled. 'Send word to Rod McKendrick, please. Tell him St George is at the Rassiter.' He looked at the key. 'Room thirty-three. At his leisure.' He shouldered his saddle-bags and turned toward the stairway. 'Don't forget the person with connections to the fairer sex,' he said over his shoulder.

Rod McKendrick wasn't used to moving at someone else's command, but he also knew that Kensington St George would not condescend to walk to the Dominion Mine's headquarters, although it was no more than a quarter of a mile away from the Rassiter. So he put on a hat, shrugged into a somber black frock coat, and marched to the hotel, Williams scurrying in his wake.

'Kensington St George?' he asked the clerk.

'Room thirty-three, sir.'

McKendrick clomped up the stairs to the third floor. Only four suites, each with sitting room and bedroom, as well as an inside water closet. He ground his teeth to think how much the suite would cost Dominion. He knocked on the door.

A rustle inside. 'The door's unlocked.'

McKendrick opened the door.

St George sat on the divan across the room from the door, a Colt Lightning .38 in his right hand, the sawed-off Parker Bros in his left.

'You live high on the hog, Ken,' McKendrick said.

St George smiled. 'In my business, a man must take what he can get. When you send word for me to come, I assume you're proffering the very best.' His smile widened. 'Would you care for some Madeira?'

'When you've heard what I have to say.'

St George put the bottle of Madeira on the little table in front of the divan. 'At least sit down, Rod. I don't like it when you stand over me.'

'Of course.' McKendrick sat in the easy chair across the low table from St George. He had yet to smile.

'Rod, I spent ten days on the back of my gawdawful mare, just because you called. Now if that's not friendship, I don't know what is.'

'You're not even friends with your own brother.'

'He's an asshole. You're not.'

McKendrick snorted, a hint of a smile showing on his face. 'That depends on whom you ask,' he said.

St George took a sip of the amber wine in his glass. 'Now. Why are you so anxious for me to come all the way to god-forsaken Mother Lode?'

'Besides Dutch Regan, you're better at finding people than anyone I know. I need you to find a man for me.'

St George lifted his glass. 'That's my business, part of it at least. Who?'

'Stan Ruggart.'

'Who's he?'

'He owns a fourth share of Dominion, but no one seems to know where he is. I need him. Mine business.'

'Find him. That's all?'

'I have a letter for him. I'd hope he'll be in contact once he's read it.'

'You want me to deliver your mail?' St George's lips lifted. Almost a sneer, but not quite.

'Ken. You know I'm aware of your status. But you're the best manhunter in the business. Ordinarily, you'd hunt the man for the price on his head, dead or alive. I'll give you five thousand to find Stan Ruggart. And I want him alive.'

Stryker and Tom Hall rode due south from Rimrock. While a wagon road wound down off the rim and through Oak Creek Canyon, Stryker chose a trail that followed Granite Creek. On the third day, Stryker reined his Arabian stallion Saif across the creek and into a little wash that ran east and just north of Granite.

'Don't like it when people show up on my back trail,' Stryker said. ' 'Specially when they're trying like hell to keep me from catching on to them.'

'I was about to mention that,' Hall said, 'but I figured

you'd pick 'em up.'

'I caught their sign,' Stryker said. 'Thing is, I haven't got the slightest notion as to why they'd want to follow us.'

Hall grinned. 'Long as you've been lawing and bounty hunting, Stryker, who'd know why someone'd want to kill you? Right now, it's enough to know those jaspers are out there. Who cares why?'

Stryker led on until the wash made a sharp jag to the southeast. He stopped Saif by a rock and climbed from the saddle on to a boulder, rifle in hand. 'Take my horse and ride on up the wash a ways,' he said. He handed the reins to Hall and said, 'Go Saif.'

Soon Hall and Saif were out of sight. Stryker climbed up the side of the gully and found a lookout in a nest of jumbled sandstone. He hunkered down to wait.

The sun burned hot and dry. Though late spring in the high Arizona country was not known for killer heat, the nest amongst the sandstone caught reflected rays and Stryker soon wished for a cedar or some scrub oak for shade. He pulled his straight-brimmed hat lower over his eyes and settled in. It might be an hour. It might be two or three. But sometime, sooner or later, those on his back trail would show themselves.

As he waited he thought about Stan Ruggart's letter. He'd not opened the will. He'd let the judge in Prescott do that. Who'd want Stan dead? Who stood to gain? His former wife Elizabeth? What was her nickname? Lizzimae? The daughter? Who hated Stan? He was a drunk, but not a belligerent one. He laughed a lot, even at himself. Stryker found no answers, but decided to look Lizzimae up once the will was probated.

Sand trickled against a rock behind Stryker. He put a hand on his Remington and started to turn.

'Don't do it, Marshal. We'uns's holding a gun on you.'

'Damn,' Stryker said. 'I shoulda known it was you. Can I turn around? I'll leave the gun alone.'

'Your word?'

'My word.'

'OK, but take it easy. Lean the Winchester against the rock. Fast moves make we'uns nervous. Besides, if we'un is to bring you in dead, we gets lots of cash money.'

'How much?'

'We'uns heared five hundred, but mebbe whomsoever's putting up the cash money'll go even higher.'

'Now Squirly. Who'd want me that dead? I'm gonna turn around now. Don't you get itchy with that trigger finger, all right?'

'Like we'uns says. Just take it easy, Marshal.'

Stryker turned to face the mousey man who held a monstrous Colt Dragoon in his small, childlike hand. 'By yourself?' he asked.

'You joshing? Don't nobody go after Matt Stryker by his lonesome.'

'Who's your partner, then?'

'We'uns got partners. Injun Jake and Wildman Kelly.'

'Sheesh. How in hell did you sneak up on me?'

'Just did it.'

'How do you figure to collect? I ain't dead.' Stryker started to put his hand into a coat pocket, but Squirly cocked the Dragoon.

'Don't you'all be making any funny moves, Marshal. I can drill you plumb through if we'uns got to.'

Stryker relaxed his hand. 'Reckon you know I'm not by myself.'

'Them others, my pards, they're collecting up your pard.'

Stryker said nothing more. It bothered him that a boy-man like Squirly Adams could slip up on him, but that was that and he decided to wait until Tom Hall and Squirly's 'pards' came.

'Stryker?' Hall's call came from up the wash.

'Mind if I answer?' Stryker deferred to Squirly.

'Just don't do nothing funny.'

Stryker raised his voice. 'I'm here, Tom.'

'What's going on?'

'Old friend come to call.'

'I'll bet. Two of his *compadres* here with me.'

'Let's parley with them, Tom.' Stryker shot a glance at Squirly, who had what Stryker thought of as a shit-eating grin on his face. 'What's your plan, Squirly?'

'Like you say, Marshal, let's parley. How about we go down and meet 'em?'

'You're gonna climb down the rocks with that cannon in your hand?'

'You gave your word.'

Stryker gave Squirly a stony look. 'Yes, I did.'

'Then we'uns'll go down.' Squirly let the Dragoon's hammer down and shoved the gun behind his waistband. 'Come on.'

Squirly led the way, jumping from rock to rock like a twelve-year-old. Stryker followed, taking much more care. A broken leg would help no one. Hall, two other riders, and five horses came walking down the wash as Squirly and Stryker reached the bottom.

A cutaway where flash floods had carved up the sandstone side of the wash threw a bit of shade. Stryker waved a hand at it. 'Why not hunker down in the shade while we talk,' he said. 'Maybe build a fire and brew some coffee. Reckon we could to that, Jake?'

'Ain't nobody near but us,' said the dark man to Tom's left. He wore a turkey feather in his floppy felt hat and Apache moccasins that reached nearly to his knees.

'Heard you ran with Apache Kid,' Stryker said.

'Nah. He likes to kill and kill and kill. Kill too much and you die too soon.' A touch of mirth showed in the half-breed's eyes.

'You're a smart man, Jake. Man can't do nothing when he's dead,' Stryker said. 'Squirly, you reckon you could make us a little fire over there by the cutaway? I'll get the fixings off my horse.'

'You just gonna sit back and chew the fat with these. . . .' Hall couldn't come up with the right word to describe the three misfits who'd come hunting the reward for Matt Stryker's death.

'Take it easy, Tom,' Stryker said. 'Just take it easy. Things'll work out. You'll see.'

Squirly gathered juniper sticks and pine needles to put together a little fire. Stryker got his four-cup coffee pot and a little sack of Arbuckle's coffee beans. 'You know how to crush beans, Jake?' he asked.

The half-breed snorted. 'I been doing the bean crushing since I can remember,' he said. 'When we had beans.'

Stryker handed him the sack. 'Pound up enough for four cups, Jake. That's all my pot will make.'

Injun Jake took the beans and went in search of a flat rock. Stryker poured water into the coffee pot and set it by the fire. 'Damn fine day,' he said, looking up at the blue sky. A few cottonball clouds floated, but otherwise the heavens were absolutely clear. 'Reckon it'll rain?' he said.

'Oh, no, Marshal,' said Squirly, his face serious. 'Clouds is different when the rains come. We'uns seen 'em before.'

'You're probably right. I just felt a twinge in my sacroiliac, and sometimes that means rain.' He struggled to keep a straight face. He glanced at Tom Hall, who wore a look of incredulity and obviously didn't know what the hell was going on.

Injun Jake came back with a handful of pounded coffee

57

beans. 'In the pot?' he said.

'In the pot,' Stryker said.

Stryker leaned against the sandstone wall of the cutaway, letting his body soak up some of the cool from the rock. Saif the Arabian stallion watched Stryker's every move. Hall hunkered down on his heels, back against the cutaway. Injun Jake sat cross-legged in the shadow and Wildman Kelly squatted beside him. Squirly paced back and forth in front of the fire.

The pot frothed.

'Squirly, I'm going to pull my knife and tap the pot,' Stryker said.

Squirly nodded.

Stryker took his Bowie by the handle and tapped the coffee pot with the heavy blade. 'That'll settle the grounds,' he said. 'Get your cups.'

No one moved.

He looked around. 'No one wants coffee?'

'Ain't got no cups,' Squirly said.

'Shee-it. What the hell are you doing out here without a coffee cup?' He made it sound like a capital offense.

Squirly scrubbed a toe in the dirt and changed the subject. 'You owe me a dollar, Jake,' he said.

'We'll take turns,' Stryker said. 'I'll get my cup. Tom?'

'Me, too,' Hall said.

'A dollar,' Squirly said.

'Yeah yeah. You'll get your damn dollar,' Jake said.

Wildman sat and stared at the fire.

7

Elizabeth Wharton wanted it all. She'd given Stanford Ruggart a snot-nosed kid, a girl she didn't really care for. So she'd smacked the brat a couple of times. How was that grounds for divorce? Lizzimae didn't want a divorce anyway. All she wanted was everything Stan Ruggart had. She'd get it, too, if she had to kill him. A wife automatically inherits her husband's property – and that includes money – when he dies.

Lizzimae's preacher father taught her right from wrong and all about the evils of hard liquor. Unfortunately, the lessons about the effects of whiskey came first hand, because Preacher Wharton kept a jug in the barn, and he liked his young daughter's flesh a lot more than the favors of his scarecrow wife. Stan Ruggart drank hard, too, but he never laid a hand on Lizzimae after drinking. Maybe that's why she hated him so.

After she'd walked out on Ruggart she worked saloons, looking for just the right man to tie up with. To get Ruggart's fortune, she'd need a good partner. First she got a job at the Black Diamond in Ehrenburg. The Diamond was the first place she was able to gather her wits after bolting from Mother Lode in the middle of the night, Stan Ruggart having passed out on the parlor floor.

The Black Diamond saw a constant stream of men who'd stopped to clear their throats of trail dust, usually with house whiskey, a combination of grain alcohol, chilli peppers for bite, chewing tobacco for color, and rattlesnake heads for the hell of it. Lizzie didn't find her partner there, so she moved on to Vulture City, where the Vulture mine put out more gold than any operation east of Sutter's Mill.

The Carrion was the biggest saloon in Vulture City, and Lizzimae soon pushed drinks and pleasured miners and cowpokes when the man or the money was right.

She spotted Virgil Teague the minute he stepped through the Carrion's batwings. When he reached the bar, Lizzimae was there. 'Hi, mister. Buy a poor girl a drink?' she simpered. All she got from Teague was a stony stare.

Lizzimae changed tacks. 'You look like the kind of man I need,' she said. 'Could we have a little conversation? Just you and me?' The simper was gone from her voice. It now carried a flinty edge that matched Teague's stare.

He ignored her. 'I'll have a bottle of Old Grand-Dad and a clean glass,' he said to the bartender.

'Ten dollars,' the barkeep said.

Teague put an eagle on the bar. 'I said a *clean* glass.' His voice still sounded like a hard rock.

'Could mean a lot of money,' Lizzimae said.

Teague condescended to look down at her. 'And what makes you think I need money, whore?'

She smiled sweetly. 'I fuck like you'd never believe, big man, but we're talking about a different kind of hole. One filled with silver, and even a big, rich man like you knows that money buys power.' She turned her back on him and threaded her way through the tables to an empty one, where she sat, her back straight and her hands clasped primly in her lap.

Teague drank the first shot of Old Grand-Dad standing at

the bar. He looked at Lizzimae in the bar mirror. She sat prim and alone at the table. A cowboy sloped by and said something to her. She said something back, and the cowboy walked away, shaking his head. Teague downed a second shot.

When the bottle was down by a third, Lizzimae still sat primly at the empty table. She'd refused to talk to any man who happened by, though her dress and her makeup said she should be available.

Rather than saloon women, Teague preferred the genteel atmosphere of Miss Allison's Finishing School for Young Ladies, where women dressed and undressed in impeccable fashion and made every man feel special. Saloon girls, Teague knew, never wore underwear, hiked their skirts and bared their bottoms in bed, coupling with cowboy, miner, and drummer alike, most of whom didn't do more than unbutton their pants to take their poke. What's more, the chance of catching the clap was somewhere around fifty-fifty. He gulped another shot of Old Grand-Dad and studied the woman in the bar mirror.

Silver. A hole full of silver. That could only mean a mine. Nevada? California? Teague had not heard of silver in Arizona. For a moment he considered the Vulture mine. No way to get it. Belton Phelps had it tied down. Silver. Not gold, but still . . . worth a lot. He looked in the mirror. The woman refused another customer, a miner by his clothes.

'Another glass, please,' he said when the barkeep wandered by, wiping the gleaming bar down with a wet cloth.

'Here you go,' the 'keep said, taking a glass from a stack on the back counter and putting it in front of Teague. 'Need me to call anyone for you?' he asked.

'Thank you, no,' Teague said. He picked up the two glasses in one hand, the bottle in the other, and made his way to Lizzimae's table.

'Yes, I'd love a drink,' Lizzimae said before Teague could say a word. 'Please sit down and make yourself comfortable.'

Teague sat and poured her two fingers of bourbon. He raised an eyebrow. 'You said something of silver.'

Lizzimae nodded. 'Thank you for the whiskey,' she said. She took the glass with dainty fingers, but her pull on the liquor was more hard-rock miner than frilly lady. She put the glass down and sighed. 'Yes, silver,' she said.

'Why me?' he asked.

'Hunger.'

'What do you mean. I've not gone hungry in years.' Teague sipped at his whiskey.

'Oh, but you're hungry. Really hungry. Not for a beef-steak, though,' she said. 'You're the kind of man who's hungry for power. Pure bloody power.'

Teague smiled.

Lizzimae took another slug of whiskey. 'So why are you here, then?'

'As I said, I heard talk of silver. Next to gold, silver is a favorite of mine. Talk.'

'Ever heard of Mother Lode?'

'That town's way the hell up on the mountain. Who knows if it's California or Nevada. Colder than a witch's tit, I've heard. Town built on silver, they say.'

'I could own one of those mines.'

'Could?'

'Right now, I'm just the wife, but if a certain man was to die, I'd be owner.'

Teague's eyes sharpened. 'Are you suggesting that I kill someone for you?'

'You don't have to do it yourself.'

'If I kill this . . . someone, then you're an owner and I'm a killer.'

'No. You'd be a partner.'

Teague sipped at his Old Grand-Dad, but he had nearly half a bottle in his gut and Lizzimae was starting to look quite desirable. 'How do we seal the deal?' he asked.

'Handshake,' she said.

'Aren't there plans to be made? Things to be discussed in private?'

'You want to fuck?'

Teague gave her a long look. 'That did cross my mind, though I would not speak to a lady in so crass a manner,' he said.

Lizzimae laughed, her voice shrill with Old Grand-Dad bourbon. 'I'm no lady,' she said. 'I'm a gold-digging whore . . . or silver-digging, in this case.' She turned stone-serious. 'Are you in?'

'Let's just say I'm very interested,' Teague said. 'Right now I don't have enough information to make a decision one way or the other.'

'Let's go fuck,' Lizzimae said. 'Then I'll tell you all about the Dominion mine in Mother Lode, Nevada.' She stood to go. 'Bring the bottle,' she said, and walked, hips swaying, toward the stairway.

Teague took the bottle of Old Grand-Dad in one hand, the glasses in the other, and followed Lizzimae. He could always back out if the deal turned sour.

He found Lizzimae even more passionate than he'd imagined. He'd not thought three couplings were possible in forty-five minutes, but somehow Lizzimae coaxed it out of him, despite most of a bottle of Old Grand-Dad.

'I think I'll be glad to have you around, partner,' she said, her face deadpan serious.

'We're out of Old Grand-Dad,' he said.

'Stan Ruggart's got to die,' she said.

'Far from here, I suppose?'

'He's in Rimrock right now.'

'Rimrock's mine's played out. What's he doing there?'

'I have no idea, but probably drinking himself to death.'

'Then why bother?' Teague sat up and lowered his feet to the rag rug on the floor.

'I want all he's got. He owes me.' Lizzimae ran a finger down Teague's spine. 'Are you going somewhere?'

'I saw a card game downstairs. I reckon it's time to earn my keep.' He walked to the high-back chair where he'd left his clothes, and began to dress.

'How're we going to kill him?'

'May be best that you don't know. But it'll take cash to get the job done.' Teague shrugged into his shirt, buttoned it, tucked the tail in his trousers, and pulled the suspenders up over his shoulders.

Lizzimae sat silent, a thoughtful look on her face. 'How much?' she said.

'You'd better figure on a thousand,' he said. 'May not go that high, but then again, it may go more.'

'OK,' she said, and she stayed in the room while Teague went downstairs to gamble. She had no doubt he would do well. She knew that the miners of Vulture City often spent much more than hard-rock diggers should be able to, but then, some were very astute at high grading.

She wiped her body down with a washcloth moistened in water from the commode. From her possibles bag, she took a small vial of lavender water and splashed a bit between her breasts, rubbed it in well with the balls of her fingers, and then dabbed a smidgen of the scent behind her ears. Teague might want to romp again later, and Lizzimae liked to be ready. Not a man in the world that didn't like the smell of lavender on a woman's skin.

'We'll kill Stan Ruggart,' she said to the mirror, 'and then I'll have more money than God.' She locked the door as she left, and took her time descending the stairs. She knew she looked good, and she milked her entrance for all she could get.

Teague ignored her, concentrating on the cards.

'Your Lady Luck has arrived,' she said in her most seductive, throaty voice.

Teague didn't look up.

She put a hand on his shoulder.

He laid his cards face down on the table and removed her hand. He stood and turned slowly. 'This may look like a game to you, but it's dead serious business to me. I'll thank you for not interrupting my train of thought. Now. If you don't mind. I'll turn my attention to the cards.' He sat and picked up his hand. 'Shall we continue, gentlemen,' he said.

Lizzimae watched for a while, then wandered off to the bar. She did notice, however, that the pile of chips in front of Teague had grown significantly. He wasn't kidding about earning his keep.

She talked to Jase the bartender whenever he wasn't serving drinks. Then she sauntered over to the upright and drummed her fingers in time with *A Rollicking Band of Pirates, We.*

'Wanna sing?' Black Willy asked.

She shook her head. 'Killing time,' she said, waving in the direction of the poker game.

Black Willy played three bars of *Camptown Races.* 'Ain't nobody wins in them games,' he said. 'And plenty of peoples die.' He shook his head and started playing *Drink to Me Only with Thine Eyes.*

In the wee hours the Carrion quieted down. The miners needed a little sleep before the day shift began. Black Willy quit playing the upright and disappeared into the back of the saloon. Jase sat on a stool behind the bar, his eyes closed and his chin on his chest. The doves had either found a sweet daddy for the night or slouched away to wherever soiled birds roost. Lizzimae sat at an empty table with her forehead on her arms. At the card game the players were down to two plus the house dealer. Teague had piles of chips on the table before him. The other player, a well-dressed man in a rancher's Stetson, had only a few. The dealer only handled the cards; he wasn't allowed to bet.

'New deck, if you please,' Teague said.

The dealer got up to fetch the new cards from behind the bar.

'You're a lucky son of a bitch,' the rancher growled.

Teague smiled. 'You learn to play the odds, Mr Smith,' he said, although he didn't think for a minute that the man's name was actually Smith. 'Some hands are better than others, and with some you just try to make the best of it.'

'My ass,' the rancher said.

'No need to be crude, Mr Smith.'

The dealer returned, broke open the new pack and shuffled the fifty-two pasteboards. 'Five-card draw?' he asked as part of the ceremony of opening a new deck of cards.

'Same game,' Smith said, scowling.

Teague nodded.

Smith anted up a twenty-dollar chip. Teague matched him.

Alternating, the dealer dealt each player a card, face down, until five cards lay before Teague and Smith.

Teague decided to end the game. Without looking at his cards, he pushed a pile of chips to the center. 'Five hundred dollars,' he said.

'You know I don't have that much,' Smith said.

'Yes, I know. Would you like to bet your ranch? I'll lend you a thousand dollars against its title.'

Smith threw in his hand, scattering the cards across the table. 'You've been chipping away all night, Teague. Ain't no man on earth that lucky.'

Teague gave a thin smile that came nowhere near his eyes. 'Are you intimating that my poker skills may be under-handed?'

'Didn't say that,' Smith said. 'But the air around here has a certain foul odor.'

Teague dug in the inner pocket for a thin cigar like the others he'd smoked during the card game. But when his hand reappeared it held a Hopkins & Allen XL revolver with a cut-down barrel and five-shot cylinder.

'Be specific, Mr Smith. Either you're saying I'm a cheat or you're just leaving after an evening spent at your favorite pastime. Which will it be? Further, understand that any claim toward my being a liar and a cheat besmirches my character, and only a barrage of 32-caliber lead will assuage the injury to my pride.'

Smith sat, looking at Teague's little revolver, his mouth working like a carp just pulled from the water.

'What will it be, Mr Smith?' Teague thumbed the hammer back for emphasis, as the double-action revolver didn't have to be cocked to fire.

'I was just leaving,' Smith said. 'Not cheerfully, but leaving.'

'An enjoyable game, Mr Smith. I'll be happy to join you any time you wish to spend a few hours at the cards of chance.' Teague eased down the hammer of the XL and returned it to the hideaway holster in his coat.

Teague nodded to the dealer. 'Thank you, Mr Whitlock,' he said. He shoved five twenty-dollar chips across the table. 'Have a drink on me.'

Smith looked at the chips in front of Whitlock, then searched Teague's face. 'You guys in cahoots?' he asked.

Teague smiled his humorless smile. 'Not at all,' he said. 'If Mr Whitlock were allowed to play, we'd both walk out of the Carrion with empty pockets. I'm just showing my

67

appreciation for a game fairly dealt, that's all.'

'Shee-it,' Smith said. He pushed his chair back and stood up. 'Don't like it,' he said, and walked away.

Just before he reached the door, the man who called himself Smith wheeled. 'You're a goldam cheat, Teague,' he hollered. As he shouted, he clawed for the Colt .45 at his belt. He had the old Colt up and firing in less than a second, but Teague was a hair's breadth ahead of him.

Teague had the little XL out in less than a heartbeat, and holding it with both hands, he pulled the trigger five times. Smith's two shots went wide, but three of Teague's little bullets hit Smith. He went down, bleeding but not dead. 'I'm not a cheat,' Teague said. He popped the empties from the gun, reloaded with the loose cartridges he carried in his right coat pocket, and put a finger to the rim of his hat to salute Whitlock, 'Cash in my chips?'

'Sure,' Whitlock said. 'Hey Jase. Cash in Mr Teague's chips for him, OK?'

Jase came and gathered up the chips without saying a word. On the floor near the door, Smith groaned. Teague went over to look at him. 'You'll live, Smith. You're not even bleeding that bad. Just be careful who you call a cheater from now on.'

'Your cash, Mr Teague.' Jase held out a sheaf of bills.

'Thank you.' Teague peeled off a twenty and handed it to Jase. 'Buy yourself a drink,' he said.

'Yeah,' Jase said. 'I'll use it wisely.'

'Lizzimae, my dear.'

Lizzimae'd ignored the gunshots, but the mention of her name caught her attention. Her head came up. 'Yes?' she said.

'Breakfast or bed, my dear?'

She looked out the window to see the day beginning to gray. 'Sun's coming up,' she said. 'We might as well get something to eat.'

'Come, then.' Teague extended his arm, and Lizzimae tucked her hand behind his elbow. They started for the door and stepped around the groaning Smith on the way out. 'After breakfast,' Teague said, 'we can think on how and where to find the barber.'

8

Five men sat in the shade of a cutaway overhang south and east of Granite Creek and drank four cups of coffee from two tin cups. The hot, dry sun climbed higher and the red-orange sandstone bleached to pink in the sunshine. None of the men spoke during the ritual-like drinking of the coffee. All wore weapons, but Matt Stryker had given his word there'd be no gunwork while they talked.

'Want to tell me what this is all about, Squirly? And don't give me lies about lots of money put on my head,' Stryker said.

'There's lots of money sitting on your head, Marshal,' Squirly said.

'You forgot about Fools Hollow already?'

Squirly squirmed. 'Ain't,' he said. 'That's kinda why we'uns come along behind you.'

'How does sneaking up on me and shoving that Dragoon in my face remind you of Fools Hollow?'

'No way we could just ride up on you, Marshal. Not with Wildman tagging along. Had to sneak up, get the drop on you, make you promise to listen.'

'I'm listening.'

Squirly stirred the coals of the little fire they'd used to brew the coffee. 'Not looking for money, Marshal,' he said in

70

a small voice.

Stryker heaved a sigh. 'Then what in hell are you doing here?'

'You go, and there ain't no reason for me to stay in Rimrock no longer,' Squirly said. 'And Injun Jake bet me a dollar I couldn't get the drop on you.' The boy-man smiled, a tentative look in his eyes. 'I won,' he said.

'What's that got to do with someone paying to have me killed?'

'Good reason to catch up with you. Good reason for you to listen. We'uns got something to say after all.'

'I wonder what it is.' Stryker's tone was flat and hard.

'Well, it's something, we'uns figure. It surely is.' Squirly looked up at Stryker, his little eyes wide and his broad smile showing small, pointed teeth.

Stryker's face could have been made of stone. He said nothing.

'Tell you what, Marshal. Me and Injun Jake was up in the loft at the livery, you know. It's a good place to catch a wink or two without we're in someone's way.'

Stryker nodded, showing Squirly he was listening.

'Ruben went over to Goldfinch's store or somewhere so it was real quiet. I could even hear horses chewing their oats, it was so quiet.'

Stryker folded his arms, his face still stern.

'Then two peoples come back.'

'Come back?'

'Yeah. Come back. It was the big one's horse what was chewing the oats. They was talking. Well, one of them was talking. He handed a pile of clothes to the big one and told him to put 'em on. I could see 'em over the edge of the hayloft. The one that were talking were just a little fellow, not much bigger'n me. And he were saying to the big one that new stuff would keep people in town from telling him

71

apart. Yeah, that's what he said.'

'Get to the point, Squirly.'

'Well, the little one gives the big one a piece of paper and some gold. I seen it shine. It were gold. And he said it were half what the big one would get for doing Matt Stryker in. Said you was worth five hundred dollars dead.'

'I know that, Squirly.'

'Here's what's funny, Marshal. After the big one left, the little one went back under the loft wheres we couldn't see. And he never come out.'

'Where'd he go?'

'God only knows,' Squirly said in his deepest voice.

'You don't have to imitate the parson.'

'Anyway, we'uns, me and Injun Jake, we climbed down from the loft after a while, but the little one was gone. And the carriage that were parked out back were gone, too. Then Ruben come back and we asked him who the young feller driving the carriage were and he said, what young feller. He said Miss Melanie Powers were the only one driving that carriage. That's what he said, and we'uns figured you'd want to know about a little man who turns into a woman, and here we is.'

It clicked. The young fellow who brought clothes at the general store was Melanie Powers. Powers. Powers. Ah, Clayton Powers. Five years ago? Six? The first bounty Stryker had hunted was Clayton Powers. Young hothead. Part of Bloody Bill's irregulars in the war. Fourteen, fifteen then. Twenty-three when Stryker caught up with him. There'd been a five-hundred-dollar bounty on Powers. He wouldn't come peacefully, so Stryker brought him in belly down over his own horse.

'You done good, Squirly. You're right that I'd want to know about the Powers woman, but the news ain't worth five hundred to me,' Stryker said.

72

'Carriage went south, Marshal,' Injun Jake said. 'Right down Black Canyon road. To my mind, that leads to Prescott.'

'It does. And that's where I'm going,' Stryker said. 'Maybe we'll meet up.'

'I'll go ahead,' Jake said. 'No one pays no attention to a tame Indian.'

'Me'n Wildman'll stick with you, Marshal,' Squirly said.

'Jayzus!' Hall looked from Jake to Squirly to Stryker and back. 'You surely ain't gonna let these . . . these. . . .' Again, Hall couldn't find a word that fit.

'Free country,' Stryker said. He fished an eagle from his pocket and held it out to Squirly. 'Thanks for the information,' he said.

Squirly grinned and took the coin. 'Welcome,' he said.

'Scouting money,' Stryker said, and handed an eagle to Injun Jake.

Jake took the coin, bit it, and nodded. 'Good,' he said.

Stryker put on his stern face. 'What about Wildman?'

'He's with me,' Squirly said. 'He goes wild again if I don't take care of him.'

Stryker looked at Wildman, who looked at the remains of the fire. He dug a third eagle from his pocket and gave it to Squirly. 'For Wildman,' he said. 'You take good care of him, y'hear?'

Squirly beamed. 'I'll do that, Marshal. Shouldn't we'uns hit the trail for Prescott?'

'Put out the fire, Squirly, and we'll go. Jake, you're out front. Tom, if you would, you can flank us. The rest of us will be along directly.' Stryker gathered up the reins of his Arabian stallion and turned him around. 'Hand me the coffee pot, Squirly. And the cups, if you please.'

Hall took his own cup, and Squirly turned the empty coffee pot upside down over the dying fire. A few drops rolled out and hissed when they hit the coals. There was no place to wash the utensils so he handed them to Stryker as they were.

Injun Jake mounted a strawberry appaloosa and wiggled his butt comfortable on the saddle. His stirrups were set long, like the Mescalero scouts at Camp Verde.

'I'm off, Marshal. Let you know if I come across anything unseemly.' He reined the strawberry down the wash toward the Granite Creek trail.

Squirly kicked sand over the fire and tromped on it. 'Come on, Wildman,' he said, 'We'll go get us something real good over to Prescott. I promise.'

Wildman looked up, a smile on his face and a bit of drool on his lips. 'Cake?' he said. 'Bear sign? Hard canny?'

Squirly took him by the hand and urged him to stand up. Then he led him to the gentle-looking bay mare and helped him into the saddle. 'You wait now, Wildman. I gotta get on my horse, too.' He took the reins to a buckskin gelding and climbed aboard. 'Come on,' he said to Wildman, and rode after Injun Jake.

Once on the trail, Stryker led with Wildman behind and Squirly in the rear. Once he stopped to check the back trail.

'Ain't nobody coming up behind us, Marshal,' Squirly said.

'How do you know?'

'Wildman'd smell 'em. An' he'd let me know.'

Stryker raised an eyebrow. 'OK,' he said after a minute. 'You let me know if Wildman catches anything coming.'

'We'uns can do that, Marshal. Mighty glad to help out.'

Stryker put Saif on the Granite Creek trail again, and they made a good twelve miles by sundown.

Injun Jake waited where a little stream trickled into Granite Creek from the east. 'Good camping up the hill a ways,' he said.

'Lead on,' Stryker said.

Jake took them nearly a mile into the foothills to where the stream had its beginnings as a spring. A low cliff formed a quarter circle back of the pool the spring bubbled into. There was plenty of browse for the horses and needles from the ponderosas back against the cliff for beds. Jake used rocks to build a little fireplace under the overhang of a sycamore. Wildman wandered off.

'Where's he going?' Stryker asked.

'Who? Wildman? Maybe to piss. But I reckon he smells something to eat.'

Hall rode in on his brown appaloosa. 'Be nice if you'd tell a man where you're going,' he said.

Jake looked up. 'Tom Hall knows how to read a trail,' he said. 'I know that. No need to treat you like a shavetail.'

Hmmph.' Hall dismounted, undid his saddle cinch, and pulled his saddle off the appaloosa. He put the gear in a likely place, then removed the horse's bridle. 'Get outta here,' he said. 'Go fill your belly with sweet grass. And let me know when you see something.' The horse nodded as if he understood every word Hall said. He walked a few steps toward the pool and started grazing.

'Damndest horse I ever seen,' Jake said. 'Where'd you pick him up?'

'Up by the Bitter Roots on the Snake,' Hall said. 'Did Chief Lawyer a favor once. Katsee was a gift.'

'Chief Lawyer? He don't give away appaloosa so easy.' Jake tipped his hat. '*Hoh*,' he said.

'*Hoh*,' said Hall, returning the Nez Percé greeting. 'You're one of the *Nimi'ipuu* then?'

'Half.'

'Fine people. Never met a *Nimi'ipuu* liar yet.'

Jake nodded. 'There are some, but straight talk is best.'

'Then I'll ask. Why you three tagging along with Stryker?'

Stryker broke up sticks for the fire that Squirly had got started, ignoring the talk between Hall and Injun Jake.

'Some folks figure the only good half-breed's a half-dead half-breed,' Jake said. 'And they don't think a half-breed's got a right to defend himself.'

'Lots depends on the half-breed, I reckon. Garet Havelock, that deputy over to Vulture City, he's half-Cherokee,' Hall said.

'I know him,' said Jake. 'Brock Harper, the man who hired Havelock, don't cotton to judging a man by his ma and pa. But Havelock's little brother Johnny's riding the Outlaw Trail.'

'Met Wolf Wilder yesterday,' Hall said.

Jake grinned. 'There's a man. White in the head, Cheyenne in the heart. Don't you ever get on the wrong side of him.'

'That don't explain why you're tagging along with Stryker.'

'I owe him.'

Hall waited for more.

'Heard people wanted him dead. I don't. So here I am. You?'

'Hired.'

'Stryker hired you?'

'Not exactly, but it kinda turned out that way. Gave my word and couldn't keep it. Watching Stryker's back kinda makes up for it.'

Jake said nothing, but searched Tom Hall's face. After some moments he said, 'He could do a lot worse.'

Tom Hall may have grinned. '*Katsee yow yow.*'

'Welcome,' Jake said.

A rustling in the brush had Tom Hall reaching for his six-gun.

Jake shook his head. 'Wildman,' he said.

76

Hall looked a bit sheepish. 'Shoulda known. A man can't be too careful, though.'

'Meat,' Wildman said. He held two cottontail rabbits by the ears.

'Good man,' Squirly said. 'Come on, we'll skin 'em.' He led Wildman Kelly aside and took out a slim skinning knife. 'Hold 'im.'

Wildman held a rabbit up by the hind legs. Squirly slit it up the front then down each leg. He made a circle around each paw and peeled the skin off up to the neck. He severed the head from the body and threw it aside, skin attached. He eviscerated the rabbit and said, 'Hold it right there, Wildman.'

'Meat,' Wildman said.

Squirly cut a thumb-thick stick from a poolside red willow, stripped the bark from it, sharpened one end, and skewered the butchered rabbit. He cut off the furry paws and handed the carcass to Stryker. 'Hold on to that piece of meat, would you, Marshal?'

Stryker complied. Squirly and Wildman butchered the other cottontail. 'Was planning on sowbelly and saleratus biscuits,' Stryker said. 'But these will do fine.'

'We'uns didn't bring no vittles,' Squirly said, 'and Wildman's right good at catching small critters.'

'Thank you, Kelly,' Stryker said.

'Meat,' said Wildman.

Squirly watched over the rabbits as they roasted on willow sticks over the fire. When the juices started to sizzle, he sprinkled the meat with some salt that Stryker gave him.

Stryker mixed two cups of flour with about a teaspoon of saleratus and a pinch of salt. The mix nearly filled his little frying pan, but a little water from the pool soon turned it into manageable dough.

'Borrow your frying pan, Tom,' he said.

Hall pulled a little pan from his saddle-bag. 'You can use it if you give me some of the bread,' he said, a grin on his face.

Stryker smiled. 'You should be so lucky. Won't take but a minute.'

Stryker put a little leftover bacon grease in Hall's pan and set it on three rocks positioned to hold it over one side of the fire. Scooping dough from his own pan with three fingers, he plopped each biscuit in the frying pan. The heat made the dough rise, and soon five plump biscuits filled the pan.

Squirly turned the rabbits and the smell of roasting meat rose from the fire. Injun Jake slipped away. Stryker turned the biscuits over.

When the rabbit meat was stripped from the carcasses and fit between biscuits to make hefty sandwiches, Jake came back. Stryker started another mess of biscuits in Hall's frying pan.

'Anything out there?' Hall asked.

Jake shook his head.

'Meat. Bread.' Wildman sank his big teeth into a saleratus biscuit and roast-rabbit sandwich.

Stryker held his sandwich up. 'Thank you for the meat, Kelly,' he said.

Wildman mumbled, his mouth full, and nodded his head vigorously.

When they'd finished Squirly threw the remains of the rabbits out where the varmints could get to them. Then he washed the utensils in the pool. They stood around, passing the two coffee cups back and forth. 'There ain't nothing that can beat a good meal,' Jake said. 'Not even store-bought whiskey.'

'Good,' Wildman said.

'You stay awake first, Jake, if you would. Wake Tom

around midnight. And Tom, you can wake me at four. Got a watch?'

Hall patted his vest pocket.

'Good. Squirly, you can take care of the fire.'

'Right, Marshal. Um, Marshal. . . .'

Stryker looked up from where he was putting the frying pan back into his saddle-bags. 'Say it, Squirly,' he said.

'Well, we'uns ain't got no blankets, Marshal. Could we use your and Mr Hall's saddle blankets? To go with the ones from our own horses?'

Stryker looked at Hall, who nodded. 'All right, Squirly. Go ahead.'

'We'uns'll make up your beds, too, Marshal,' Squirly said.

Wildman gathered pine needles from under the stand of ponderosas and piled them where Squirly told him to.

The night passed as hard men with wary eyes kept watch because a woman named Powers had put a price on Matt Stryker's head.

9

Whipple Barracks stood on the high ground south of Granite Creek, its whitewashed walls reflecting the evening light. Back in '63, before the nearby mining town even got the name of Prescott, Fort Whipple was capital of Arizona, and the barracks still liked spit and polish. No blue-clad soldier challenged Stryker's little platoon of riders as they passed. The trail along Granite Creek turned into a mining road that went west of the barracks and by the hogtown to the south.

'Time for a tame Indian,' Jake said.

'Keep your head down, Jake,' Stryker said.

'I been a tame Indian most of my life, Marshal. I know how it's done.' He tipped his hat. 'Let you know if I hear anything.' He broke off from the group and headed for hogtown.

Sturgis's livery stable showed on the left as the four riders reached the outskirts of town. 'Me and Wildman, we'uns'll bunk at the livery,' Squirly said. 'Ain't a livery stable ever what won't let a man sleep in the loft if he mucks out the stalls.'

'Stay out of trouble, Squirly, and take good care of Kelly,' Stryker said.

Wildman smiled when Stryker called him by name.

80

'Kelly,' he said.

Stryker and Hall rode over the bridge to Gurley Street. The light turned gold and coral as the sun slid down the side of Thumb Butte and Prescott slipped into the silver-gray of dusk.

'The only hotel I know is the Jeffrey. Is that OK with you?' Stryker asked.

'Who's paying?'

'Stan Ruggart, I reckon. We'll go see the judge in the morning.'

'Sounds good. Who do you figure knows you're in town?'

'Could be the whole county by now,' Stryker said. 'I can't hide out, you know. We're here to shake the apple tree, and who knows where the fruit will fall.'

The two men rode the wide streets of Prescott, turned left on Lincoln. Bob Brow's Palace saloon sat on the corner of Montezuma at the head of Whiskey Row. 'Hear that Palace saloon's a right fancy place for a man to get a decent shot of whiskey,' Hall said.

'We can try it once we're settled in,' Stryker said. 'Might be we should look up Tom Easter. He's marshal here and we'd better let him know what's going on, just in case.'

'You're calling the tune, Stryker. I'm just tagging along.'

The Jeffery stood on a quarter-acre one street south of Whiskey Row, three stories high with a columned porch on three sides. An oriental rug covered the pine flooring in the lobby. The counter ran from the wall to the stair landing, its mahogany burnished to a high shine. The clerk behind it sported slicked hair, parted in the middle, waxed moustache, white shirt with a bow tie and sleeve garters, and a checked vest. The Jeffery was a fine hotel to be accepting a pair of dusty riders.

'Gentlemen?' the clerk said.

'Two rooms, I reckon,' Stryker said. 'Bath?'

'Yes, sir. Rooms next to each other, then?'

'That's right. Second floor rooms. With windows.'

'Oh, yes sir. We have two vacant.' He twirled the register around on its stand. 'Signatures, gentlemen.'

Matthew Stryker wrote his name, followed by 'Rimrock, Arizona.'

Tom Hall raised his eyebrows as he read Stryker's entry. Thomas Hall, he wrote. He paused, then scribbled 'El Paso, Texas.'

'El Paso?' Stryker said.

'Last place I spent any time.'

Stryker nodded. 'Good a place as any,' he said. 'Where do we put our horses?' he asked the clerk.

'Around to the back, sir. You'll find a stable and paddock there.'

'Extra?'

'Board and hay comes with the room, sir, but it will be an extra fifty cents a day for grain, morning and night.'

'We'll want grain,' Stryker said. 'Put it on the bill for the rooms.'

The clerk put two keys on the gleaming counter. 'Rooms two thirteen and two fourteen,' he said.

Stryker hesitated a moment, then picked up the key to 213. No use trying to change his luck now. 'Bath?'

'Bathroom at the back of the hotel, sir. Enter from the north-side porch. Twenty-five cents, paid to the proprietor. It's in the hotel building, but not run by our management. Fine, clean place though, sir.'

Stryker nodded. 'We'll see to our stock,' he said.

After they took care of their horses, Stryker and Hall climbed the wide staircase in the center of the lobby. The rooms were almost to the back of the hotel as there were fifteen rooms on each side of the hallway. Hall put a hand on Stryker's arm as he started to put his key in the lock of

213. Hall held his hand out for the key. Stryker shrugged and gave it to him. Hall motioned Stryker away from the door, then stood to the right of the jamb as he inserted and turned the key with his left hand. He opened the door and went in at a crouch, his six-gun ready and cocked.

The room was dark and silent.

'Man can't be too careful,' Hall said. 'Dumb Dickie like to blew your head off, didn't he?'

'He did.' Stryker tossed his saddle-bags and blanket roll on the bed. 'I need a bath and shave and a long-ignored trip to the two-holer.' He pulled a watch from his vest pocket. 'Six and a bit,' he said. 'See you in the lobby about seven. We can get some vittles and taste some of Bob Brow's booze. Tom Easter'll be making the rounds. We can talk to him when he comes into the Palace.'

'That's the most I ever heard you say in one breath.' Hall chuckled. 'You'd better hurry or I'll beat you to the bath.' He unlocked his own room and went in.

A bath and a shave and a damp cloth taken to dusty clothes made new men of Stryker and Hall. Even the leather of their gunbelts had been wiped down. And the guns, of course.

Stryker's straight-brimmed black hat fit low across his brow. For some reason, he'd added a hatband of small silver conchos. He'd changed into a dark-red shirt the color of dried blood. His dark-grey wool trousers were brushed and rid of trail dust. They fell over black boots wiped to a shine. His Remington Army rode aslant, just behind his right hip. He'd left his coat in the room, but wore a black leather vest.

Hall was for a drink at the Palace, too. His fawn hat showed some sweat grease at the joint of crown and brim, but he'd covered most of it with a hatband of rattlesnake skin. He'd not changed shirt or trousers, but he wore a fresh-laundered red bandanna. His Colt SAA .45 sat in a light brown rig with extra bullets in a double row around his left hip. A Bowie-knife sheath looped the gunbelt on the left, handle at his left elbow. Come what might, Tom Hall was ready. 'Eat or drink?' he said.

'Both,' Stryker said. 'Hear the Palace sets a good table.'

'Sounds like my kinda place. Long as it don't cost too much.'

'Stan Ruggart's buying,' Stryker said. 'Let's go.'

They left the Jeffery, stepping off the porch into the dusty street. Half a long block put them at the end of the board-walk that ran up Montezuma Street in front of the thirty-odd saloons that made up Whiskey Row.

'Damn,' Hall said. 'Take a man more'n a day to drink his way up this street.'

'Makes a man wonder, don't it?' Stryker waved a hand at the big three-story brick building across the street. 'Governor's office in there. State legislature meets there. Yavapai County court's in there. Arizona State court, too. And what's on the other side of the street from all that pomp? More saloons than you'll find anywhere east of the Barbary Coast in San Fran. You gotta wonder why.'

'Must not be many wild drinkers.'

'You want to go wild, go to hogtown, I reckon.' Stryker managed a small smile.

The night seemed busy. Of 2,000 and some residents of Prescott, a goodly share found some reason to visit Whiskey Row. And with the city being capital of the Arizona Territory, powerful men gathered to gain more power from the courts and the legislature. Montezuma Street measured twenty-five yards, side to side, and along the block filled by Whiskey Row, traffic slowed. A steady stream of men in citified clothes moved from the capitol building to the boardwalk. Those walking toward the building were mostly alone. Those coming from it were mostly in twos and threes. Dark suits and bowler hats were the uniform of the day.

Hitching racks lined both sides of Montezuma, but those who came to drink by buggy parked their rigs aslant cross the street, leaving the teams tied to the rail there. Men who rode in for refreshment hitched their horses at the rail in front of Whiskey Row. These were men who wore Stetsons. Stryker noticed two in red and white calfskin vests. Nearly all wore six-guns.

Stryker and Hall sauntered up the boardwalk, threading through the throngs of men looking to wash away the day's dust with a shot of whiskey.

They passed Jersey Lilly's and Matt's and Hooligan's. A place called the Bird Cage promised a famous thespian would recite Shakespeare every hour on the hour from eight until midnight.

The big brick building on the corner of Montezuma and Gurley just said Palace Bar and Restaurant. The smell of good food, roasting beef, warm bread, pebble-dash gravy and maybe turkey, invited people to dine. Stryker and Hall went through the big swinging door into an oversized vestibule.

'Gentlemen? Will you be going to the bar or the restaurant?' A very large man with bulging biceps and a hint of Irish brogue in his voice met them in the vestibule.

'Bar first,' Stryker said. 'One drink, then some of your best fare to eat.'

'Very good, sir. May I hang your hardware in the cloakroom? Mr Brow does not allow patrons to enter the premises with firearms.' He held out a ham-size hand. 'Please,' he said.

Hall looked at Stryker and Stryker looked at Hall. They shrugged and unbuckled their gun rigs, buckled them again, and hung them over the Irishman's forearm.

'Thank you, gentlemen. I'll be Kincaid, sirs. At your

service. Your hardware will be returned when you leave the Palace. If you'll wait just one moment.' Kincaid went into a small room off the vestibule and returned empty handed.

'Follow me, gentlemen,' he said. He pushed through a swinging door and led Stryker and Hall into a long room with a bar down one side and a line of six tables down the other. There was no stage and no piano.

'Entertainment?' Stryker asked.

Kincaid half-turned and showed his big teeth in a smile. 'The Palace serves the best liquor in the territory, sir. I believe that's entertainment enough, don't you?'

Hall grinned. 'Surely is.'

'Enjoy yourselves, gentlemen. The restaurant is through that door.' He pointed. 'Whenever you're ready to eat.'

'Kincaid?'

'Sir?'

'I'm Matt Stryker.'

Kincaid turned to face Stryker, a question on his face.

'When Marshal Easter comes in, would you tell him I'd like a word with him, please.'

Kincaid nodded. 'I'll make sure the marshal knows you're here, sir.'

Stryker and Hall stepped to the bar.

'Would you look at them bottles,' Hall said. 'Ain't seen that many labelled ones since I was in King Fisher's place in El Paso.'

One of the three bartenders sauntered toward them, swiping a cloth down the bar as he came. 'What'll it be, gents?'

'You got Cuervo tequila?'

'Not much we don't have,' the 'keep said with a serious face and twinkling eyes.

'Limes?'

'Grown in the valley.'

86

'I'll have Cuervo, limes, and a glass of beer.'

'Right away.' The bartender looked at Stryker.

'What does Kincaid drink?'

'Jameson's. Pure Irish whiskey.'

'That's what I'll have.'

The bartender brought their drinks.

The door swung open. 'Matt Stryker. I hear you're looking for me. Who'd you go and kill now?'

'Hello to you, too, Tom. Heard you were wearing the badge in Prescott.' Stryker stuck a hand out and Tom Easter took it. A firm handshake between men who respected each other.

'This is Tom Hall, Tom.'

Tom Easter turned his hawk eyes on Hall. 'I heard that song they made up about you and Kid Swingle,' he said. 'People might mix us, having the same name and all.'

'Ever bit the truth,' Hall said with a straight face. 'Proud to be mixed up with you, Tom Easter.'

'Yeah. I'll bet. You in town for a while?'

'He's with me, Tom.'

'Tom Hall shows up in a town and people start dying,' Easter said.

'I told him the same thing in Rimrock,' Stryker said.

'Anybody die?'

'Some. Not his fault, though. That's why we're in Prescott. But I wanted to tell you people are out after my hide. Don't know if they'll try to hit me here, but there's a chance. Whatever happens, Tom, I wanted you to know I won't start anything.'

Easter pointed at Hall with his chin. 'What about him?'

'He's watching my back, Tom. And I trust him.'

'OK, Matt. Prescott's turning into a law-abiding town,' Easter said. 'But that don't mean nobody wears iron, even when you can't see it.'

Stryker's face was dead serious. 'I've got things to do in Prescott, Tom. But when they're done, I'll get out of your hair.'

Easter gave him a short nod. ' 'Preciate that, Matt. Watch yourself.'

Stryker stood silent for a moment, then lowered his voice. 'Tom, Stan Ruggart was killed in Rimrock. Throat cut after he was dead. I'd like to catch the one that done it, but first I've got to clear up Stan's last will and testament with the judge.'

'Stan Ruggart? Haven't I heard that name?'

'Could be. He rolled pretty high up to Mother Lode in Nevada at one time. In Rimrock, he was our town drunk.'

Easter brought the subject back to Hall. 'What's that got to do with him?'

'Someone hired Tom to protect Stan, but he got to Rimrock too late.'

'Someone?'

'What he said.'

'Who?'

'Can't say,' Hall said. 'Made a promise. Man's gotta stick by his promises.'

Easter's hawk eyes raked Hall again, head to toe. 'That right? You give me your word no one will die in Prescott, then?'

'No.'

Easter's eyebrows shot up. His tone turned icy. 'No?'

'You said yourself that people start to die whenever I'm in town. That may be true. But it don't start with me. Now, as Matt said, I'm here to watch his back. He can take care of whomsoever has guts enough to come at him straight on. But right now it seems someone wants Matt dead enough to pay good money to get the job done. Back in Rimrock, Dumb Dickie laid for Matt with a shotgun. That's a long answer, Marshal Easter, but "No" sums it up. Anyone comes gunning for Matt Stryker'll eat my lead. Back or front. Makes no difference.'

Easter gave Hall a long look. He met Easter's hawk eyes straight on, no flinching, no looking away. After a long moment Easter nodded. 'I hear you, Tom Hall,' he said, 'but you won't mind if I keep an eye out?'

'Help yourself. I ain't hiding.'

Kincaid stuck his head in the door. 'Marshal. Jersey Lilly's saying there's some rowdies in her place, breaking things up and such.'

'Be right there.' He turned to Matt Stryker. 'Good to see you, Matt. You have any trouble, I'd appreciate you coming to me first. If possible, that is. Tom. Do you mind me calling you Tom? No? Good. If Matt trusts you, I trust you. Plain as that. Good to know you.' He thrust a hand in Hall's direction.

'My pleasure, Marshal. I've heard the songs about Tom Easter, too.' He took Easter's hand and shook it. 'I ain't never been on the wrong side of the law, and I don't figure to start now.'

'I've got to go see what's going on at Jersey Lilly's,' Easter said. 'I'll be around.' He put a finger to his hat and left.

Hall tossed a shot of tequila, stuck a quarter of lime in his mouth and sucked the juice from it. He chased the potent drink with three gulps of beer.

'You've done that before,' Stryker said, sipping at his Jameson's.

'El Paso,' Hall said. 'Let's go get some vittles. I could eat a whole steer, I reckon. Them rabbits didn't go very far.'

Stryker drank the rest of his Irish whiskey. 'Come on,' he said, and headed for the restaurant. The double swinging doors let them enter almost abreast.

'Gentlemen?' the mâitre'd could have been the hotel

clerk's twin brother, in dress at least, except he wore a long black apron that reached from his waist to about six inches above the floor.

Stryker held up two fingers.

The mâitre'd led them to a small table far in the corner.

'Never seen a place like this before,' Hall said. 'And it sure as hell beats Charlie's joint in Rimrock. Sure Stan Ruggart's paying?'

The man at the next table pushed his chair back, rose, and approached Stryker and Hall. 'Gentlemen,' he said. 'My name is Kensington St George. I couldn't help overhearing your conversation. May I ask how you know Stanford Ruggart?'

10

'Kensington St George.' Stryker stood to greet the man-hunter. 'I've heard Dutch Regan speak of you. Says you're the best. Oh. Pardon me. I'm Matt Stryker and this is Tom Hall.'

St George raised an eyebrow. 'Imagine that,' he said. 'Matt Stryker and Tom Hall sharing the same table.'

'Come join us, if you will. Doesn't look like they've brought your order yet.'

'Capital. Capital.' St George took the chair to Stryker's left, which put a blank wall to his back. 'Bring my place setting over here,' he said to the waiter.

'Why were you asking about Stan Ruggart?' Stryker asked.

'Rod McKendrick in Mother Lode asked me to find Stanford Ruggart for him.'

'Who's he?'

'McKendrick owns most of the Dominion mine. Ruggart owns the rest. I gathered McKendrick wanted him on mine business.'

'He's dead.'

St George sat silent. 'That's very inconvenient,' he said at last. 'Rod wanted him alive.'

'We all did,' Stryker said.

'Inconvenient,' St George said again. 'Damned inconvenient. I'll have to wire the news to Mother Lode in the morning. Rod won't be happy.'

'Not much we can do about it,' Stryker said. 'Might as well enjoy the best the Palace has to offer. We dined on cottontail rabbit last night. We're hoping the roast beef here is better than that.'

'Would you like to order, then, gentlemen?' the waiter said.

'What's the choice?' Stryker asked.

'Well, sir. Beef, roasted or fried. Pork chops. Chicken, roasted or fried. Turkey, roasted. Venison, if you insist, but I must warn you. The venison came in today, and it should hang for at least two more days. My opinion, of course, sirs. Oh. And we have pan-fried trout, fresh from Granite Creek.

'Roast beef,' Hall said, 'and make sure it's not bleeding all over Hell's half acre.'

'Same,' said Stryker.

'Two roast beef, well done,' the waiter said. 'Won't be a moment.' He disappeared into the back room.

'Sure smells like roast beef in here,' Hall said. 'Got my mouth to watering.'

Stryker breathed in deeply through his nose. 'You're right, Tom. The savory scent of beef, though I detect an undercurrent of fat pork and the cluck of a Rhode Island Red.'

'Shee-it,' Hall said.

The waiter brought their food on a huge platter balanced on his splayed fingers and the point of his shoulder.

The meal proceeded in silence, except for the smacking of lips and occasional sucking sound as a stray drip of gravy got slurped into a hungry mouth.

'Coffee?'

The men nodded, mouths full. The waiter filled a fine china cup for each man and placed it on a saucer to the left of the plate.

Tom Hall mopped the last of the beef gravy from his plate with a piece of sourdough bread and popped it into his mouth. 'Some meal,' he said, the bread and gravy muffling his voice.

Stryker waved the waiter over. 'Pie?' he asked.

'Yes sir. Apple or peach. We've got almighty good carrot cake, too.'

'Carrot cake? Been more than a month of Sundays since I had carrot cake. I'll take a slice. And more coffee.'

Hall raised a finger. He swallowed, then said in a clear voice. 'Apple pie. I'll have apple pie.'

The waiter turned his eyes to Kensington St George.

'Just coffee,' St George said. 'I'm not as near starvation as these men.'

'Shee-it,' Hall said over a grin. 'Fancy man like you don't know what the word starvation means.'

St George's face grew serious. 'I spent the last three months of the war in Andersonville, Tom Hall. I'm lucky it was only three months. Seemed like no one, Yankee or Reb, likes a man named St George. Especially one who can't perform miracles.'

'Shee-it. Sorry,' Hall said. 'I was just a button and never got out of Texas until I had to run out or die.'

A layer of ice settled over the table, and Stryker had no idea how to break it. The cold remained while he ate the carrot cake and Hall got rid of his apple pie. Both men concentrated on their food while Kensington St George sipped his coffee and wore a quizzical look.

Hall wiped his mouth with the white linen napkin that came with the place setting. 'Look, St George,' he said. 'If I was off and outta line or something, well, I apologize. Matt Stryker says you're the best in the bounty business and that's good enough for me. A man's only as good as his friends and his word, I figure. Matt vouches for you, and he's gotta be the straightest man I know.' Hall stood and thrust his hand out. 'I'd like to shake your hand, Kensington St George. And I'd like you to know that you can count on me, just like you can count on Matt. Whenever and wherever you may need us.'

St George's face softened down and a small smile come to his lips. He scraped his chair back and stood to take Tom Hall's hand. 'No offense, young man,' he said, and the ice began to melt.

'More coffee, gentlemen?' the waiter asked.

All three men held out their cups. The waiter poured. The men sipped, and the cold was gone.

Matt Stryker paid for dinner. 'On Stan Ruggart,' he said.

'Not sure what you mean by that,' St George said, 'but I'll not complain.'

'Stan Ruggart asked me to do some things for him,' Stryker said, 'and he left plenty of money to cover the expenses. Stan was not a poor man, though he was Rimrock's town drunk.'

'Do things?'

'He figured someone would kill him, and he asked me to find whoever it was. And he told me to have his will probated.'

'He left a will?'

Stryker nodded. 'I'm taking it to the judge tomorrow.'

'Mind if I tell Rod McKendrick about that?'

'Not at all. Nothing can change it now.' Stryker drained his cup. 'What say, Tom? One for the road in the Palace bar? How about you, St George?'

'Ken,' St George said. 'My friends call me Ken.'

'Drink with us, then?' Stryker said.

'Not tonight, Matt. Another time.' St George threw a small salute. 'It seems my job's done, not that Rod will like

94

the outcome. Take care.' He strode to the swinging door, turned and nodded to Stryker and Hall, and pushed his way through.

'What've you heard about him?' Hall asked.

'He finds who he's looking for. Brings most in alive. Kills them if he has to. Good with guns. Better with knives. Bit of a ladies' man. Best if he's on your side in a scrap.'

Hall took a step toward the door to the bar. 'I'll have another tequila and beer, Matt. That should do me for the night. I got a feeling this is one night not to tie one on.'

Stryker grinned. 'Can't imagine you tying one on, Tom. You're too careful.'

'Could be. But let's have one more. Coming?'

'As I'm the one with Stan's purse, I reckon I'd better.'

The bar was noisier. Men bucked the tiger in the far corner. Of the two card games, one held people's attention. A young man in a bowler hat sat behind a great pile of chips. He concentrated on his cards, trying to ignore the crowd of onlookers. The dealer lit a cheroot. The kid held up two fingers. The dealer gave him two new cards and took his discarded ones.

'That's Ruel Gatlin,' Stryker said. 'I hear he's hunting Ness Havelock. Stay out of his way.'

'All I want is a drink of tequila and a little beer.'

Stryker and Hall savored their drinks, each having the same thing they'd started with. They ignored the crowd, yet stayed aware of what was going on around them.

'Thank you for your patronage, gentlemen,' Kincaid said as he returned their guns.

Stryker buckled his gunbelt around his hips, drew the Remington Army, and checked its loads. 'You drink good whiskey, Kincaid,' he said. 'Jameson's prime.'

'It is, sir. Straight from the old country. Glad you enjoyed it.'

Hall checked his Colt, returned it to the holster. 'Thanks, Kincaid,' he said. 'Top-notch place you've got here.'

Kincaid dipped his head to acknowledge Hall's comment. 'Come again, gentlemen. Please.'

Stryker led the way out.

The rifle shot came from across the street. Matt turned right on the boardwalk just as the bullet struck. It entered his abdomen below his short rib but didn't exit the other side. Stryker's Remington was out by reflex. Men scattered, running away from the line of fire. Stryker's eyes searched for a gunman among the rigs parked on the other side of Montezuma Street. Somehow he couldn't seem to focus. No more shots came. He found himself on his knees. He crumpled to the boardwalk, his right hand clenched around the butt of his Remington. He struggled for breath, his body wet with cold sweat. 'I'm hit, Tom. Hit bad.'

11

Kensington St George sent two telegrams the morning after Matt Stryker went down with a single gunshot wound to the gut. One to Rodham McKendrick, Dominion Mine, Mother Lode, Nevada, and one to Dr George Goodfellow, well known for his treatment of gunshot wounds.

Dr Goodfellow caught the first train out of Tucson, carrying his black surgeon's bag full of knives and scalpels, opium and chloroform, bandages and catgut, silk thread and a bag of tobacco. It also held two changes of underwear, some strong lye soap, and a bottle of carbolic acid. He'd eat whenever he could find a place that served food. He'd sleep wherever a hotel would take him.

The train to Los Angeles via Maricopa carried 123 steers and three passengers when it left Tucson on June 2, 1879. The day burned bright and the cholla shone like burnished gold. Spears of green came from the spikes of century plants, manzanita, and Joshua trees. Over the smell of wood smoke from the engine came the dusty dry aroma of the desert.

Dr Goodfellow took a seat near the end of the car and put his medical bag on the bench beside him. Further toward the front a tall man in a gray short-brimmed hat and a woman dressed a bit more garishly than was the fashion sat on the same forward-facing seat. He turned his mind to the patient in Prescott.

Three and a half hours from Tucson, the conductor stepped through the door between the passenger car and the caboose. 'Maricopa railway station in ten minutes,' he called, as if the car were full of passengers. 'A stagecoach is waiting just north of the tracks for those traveling to Phoenix.' He disappeared back into the caboose.

The train stopped at Maricopa in a cloud of hissing steam. The station building stood alone across the tracks from the water tower. From Maricopa, the tracks turned southwest and ran along the banks of the Gila to the bridge across the Colorado River at Yuma.

As promised, a Concord stood at the station building. The couple from the train were occupying the coach's rear seat when Dr Goodfellow climbed into the coach. The man with the gray hat held himself like a gambler, the woman like a whore. 'Goodfellow's the name,' the doctor said. 'A good day to you both.'

'Virgil Teague,' the gambler said, 'and this is Elizabeth Wharton.' He nodded at the woman.

The doctor settled his bag on the seat beside him, and kept a hand on it as if to prevent it from being stolen, or broken.

Teague pulled a silver flask from his inner coat pocket, unscrewed the cap, and took a deep swallow, never taking his eyes off Dr Goodfellow. Teague offered the flask to the doctor. 'One for the road, Doc?' he said. 'Man could use come rye to cut the smell of that foul steam engine's smoke from his throat.'

'Thank you, no, but it was civil of you to offer.'

A face of hair topped by a floppy felt hat stuck itself into the window. 'I'll be Santa Fe Sims,' the face said. 'An' I'll be handling the ribbons 'tween here and Phoenix. All aboard?'

The bright blue eyes under overhanging eyebrows flicked from one face to another. 'Awright. We'll roll.'

The coach swayed as Santa Fe climbed to the high seat. A whip cracked and the Gilmer and Salisbury stagecoach left Maricopa in a cloud of fine desert dust. The woman put a handkerchief to her face and Dr Goodfellow caught the scent of lavender.

The stage crossed the placid Salt River on Hayden's Ferry. Someone said the town's name was Tempe. The land spread hot and flat, with jumbled rock formations poking through the desert floor to the southwest and far off in the northeast. Farmers tamed the desert, using canals dug by ancient people long since gone. Phoenix town was laid out on the flat plain in precise blocks. The coach ran down Seventh Street and turned left on to Washington. Santa Fe Sims reined the teams in at an adobe building with a sign that read Gilmer and Salisbury.

'End of the road for today,' Santa Fe hollered. 'Those going to Wickenburg, stage leaves day after tomorrow. Anyone headed for Navajo Springs, they's one stage a week and it leaves here on Monday. Anyone headed for Prescott, be here by seven in the morning.'

Dr Goodfellow arrived at Gilmer and Salisbury well in advance of the 7 a.m. departure time for the Prescott-bound stagecoach. He lifted his eyebrows when he saw the gambler Teague and the painted Elizabeth in the waiting room. He recognized them with a nod, which they returned. No conversation ensued.

The gambler and the dove went first. Dr Goodfellow followed. They took the same seats they'd occupied the day before. Then another passenger arrived on a buckboard pulled by matched black mares. The driver handed her down. 'Thank you, Mr Stevenson,' she said. Her low voice resonated like music. Both Dr Goodfellow and the gambler Teague looked to see who the new passenger might be.

Santa Fe Sims was silent, for once. He opened the coach door without a word.

'Thank you,' the woman said in a melodious voice.

'Ma'am,' Sims said. The buckboard driver hoisted a steamer trunk up on top of the stagecoach.

Dr Goodfellow scooted to the far side to make room for the woman. She stepped up into the coach and took the seat the doctor had vacated. 'Thank you, sir,' she said. She adjusted her dove gray skirt, tugged at the matching waistcoat, and patted her hair to make sure it was in place. No makeup showed on her face, yet her deep-blue eyes were framed by long, dark lashes and every hair of her eyebrows seemed specially placed to enhance her beauty.

'I am Catherine de Merode,' the woman said, and settled back in her seat, hands clasped demurely in her lap.

'Dr George Goodfellow of Tucson,' the surgeon said.

'I'm Virgil Teague and this is Elizabeth Wharton,' the gambler said.

The woman's eyes seemed to narrow a fraction at the mention of the dove's name. 'A pleasure, I'm sure,' she said.

'Yeeeeee-hah.' Santa Fe Sims screamed at the teams and cracked his whip. The stagecoach lurched into motion and exited Phoenix in a dust cloud. Both the women held handkerchiefs to their noses, and Dr Goodfellow caught a mixture of lavender and lilac amidst the dust. A tiny smile crossed his lips. Travel was always so much more pleasant in the company of women.

For some miles the passengers rode in silence. Dr Goodfellow shut his eyes and leaned against the backrest, his bowler pushed down over his eyes. Catherine de Merode sat straight and prim, her hands still in her lap. Teague and the dove stuck their heads together and talked. Over the rumbling of the coach, the pounding of the horses' hoofs, and the periodic shout from Santa Fe Sims, neither the doctor nor the woman could hear what the gambler and the dove said.

They changed teams twice on the way and reached Prescott late in the afternoon. Thumb Butte towered over the town in the west. Two new buildings were going up along Black Canyon Road, skeletons of studs and beams and bare rafters. Men wielded hammers and saws, and soon the buildings would house new businesses in the booming territorial capital.

Santa Fe Sims hauled the teams to a stop in front of a low frame building with a Gilmer and Salisbury sign on the front. Corrals behind the building held dozens of big draft horses, and six-ton Murphy freight wagons stood in a line along the side of the road. Three varnished Concords with Gilmer & Salisbury painted on their doors lined the street going the other direction.

As the stagecoach braked a young man in green visor and gartered shirtsleeves stood by to open the door for the passengers. 'Dr Goodfellow,' he called.

'What is it?'

'Kensington St George has a buggy ready to take you to Dr Craig's residence, sir. If you will follow me, please.'

Dr Goodfellow followed the young man, who took his black bag and hurried the doctor to a waiting buggy. He carefully placed the bag on the floorboard and offered a hand to help the doctor up.

'I'm quite able to get into a buggy on my own,' Dr Goodfellow said, a smile taking the sting from the words.

'Yes, sir. Mr St George is waiting.'

'Let's be away, then.'

A dark young man held the reins. 'If you will, please,' the doctor said. The driver flicked the reins and the bay mare between the shafts trotted away toward Gurley Street and the heart of Prescott. The driver never took his eyes from the road and he never spoke, but Dr Goodfellow got the impression that the young man was completely aware of everything around him and more than skilful at handing the bay mare.

The buggy stopped at the white frame house fronted by a picket fence. A small sign to the right of the door said Joseph Craig MD.

'Fix Matt Stryker, Doc,' the driver said. 'You fix him, hear?'

Dr Goodfellow looked straight into the young man's Indian-dark face. 'I don't work miracles,' he said, 'but if my skills and knowledge can help, I'll use them. And if your Matt Stryker has the will to live after that, well, we'll just have to see.'

'You fix him.' The pleading was not in the young man's voice, but in his face.

'Matt Stryker's a lucky man to have friends worry over him. Could I know your name?'

The young man ducked his head. 'I ain't nobody,' he said. 'Jacob Bent's my name, but most folks just call me Injun Jake.'

'Jacob. I'll see that Matt Styker knows you are concerned about him. Now. I'd best get in to see the patient. Could you hand me the bag on the floorboard, please?'

Jake retrieved the bag and handed it to the doctor. As the doctor turned to walk to the front door Jake said, 'Help him, doc, please.'

The man who opened the door for George Goodfellow could have doubled for the late President Abraham Lincoln. He had the same tall gangly mein and he affected a beard that curled tightly from ear to ear. Like the late president, his upper lip was clean shaven, and his bony wrists protruded from shirtsleeves that seemed too short. 'Welcome,

George,' he said, thrusting out a hand.

'Joseph. And how is Evangeline?'

'Fine. Fine. It's the gut-shot man who's the problem.'

'Let's have a look.'

Dr Craig led the way to the sick room where Matt Stryker lay on a hard flat cot. Dr Goodfellow leaned over him. 'Flushed, all right,' he said. 'I'll be back in a minute. Joseph, some hot water and clean towels, please.'

'Certainly.' Dr Craig raised his voice. 'Theresa!'

'*Sí* Doctor.' A small Mexican woman entered the room.

'Hot water and towels for Dr Goodfellow, please.' He turned to Goodfellow. 'Theresa has most anything you'll need, George,' he said.

'*Jabón*, Señor Doctor?' Theresa asked.

'I have soap,' Dr Goodfellow said, 'but you'll want to bring a basin.'

Dr Goodfellow waited until Theresa brought the water, basin, and towels. After she put them on the commode Goodfellow scrubbed his hands with lye soap and dried them thoroughly with a towel. 'Now,' he said, 'let us examine the patient.'

He removed the covering sheet. 'The man walks in harm's way,' he said when he saw the scars that marked Stryker's torso. 'And I'll need to cut that bandage.' He dug into his bag for a pair of scissors and snipped through the layers of gauze wrapped around Stryker's body. The ends fell away, leaving a square pad lying directly on the wound. Gently, he lifted the pad. It stuck at one edge, then came away as the doctor gave it an extra tug. 'Hmmmm,' Dr Goodfellow said.

The entry wound was swollen, almost closed, and the flesh around the wound stood proud and red. Dr Goodfellow touched the inflamed flesh with a forefinger. 'Hot and firm,' he said.

Stryker seemed aware for the first time. 'Get the damned bullet out of me,' he croaked. 'I've been hit worse.'

Dr Goodfellow ignored Stryker. 'Joseph, the sun is almost down. What do you have in the way of lighting?'

'Hurricane lanterns. They're the brightest I've found.'

'Get them ready to light, please.'

'Certainly.' Dr Craig left the room.

Tom Hall stuck his head in. 'You Doc Goodfellow?' Without waiting for an answer, he continued. 'Heard about the cowboy you fixed up, so fix Matt Stryker. We got work to do.' He pulled his head out of the doorway, and the sound of his boots clonked across the waiting room. A chair squeaked under his weight. Dr Goodfellow lined his instruments up on the commode.

'The lamps are ready,' Dr Craig said when he returned.

'We'd better light them now.'

'I have hooks for four. Is that enough?'

'Have to be,' Dr Goodfellow said. 'Carbolic solution?'

Theresa got a large bottle from a cabinet. '*Aquí*,' she said.

'Looks like enough,' Dr Goodfellow said.

Dr Craig brought four hurricane lanterns in, hung them from hooks suspended from the ceiling, and trimmed the wicks. 'There,' he said.

'Joseph,' Dr Goodfellow said, 'I may have to open this man up wide. The size of the wound says forty caliber, probably .44-40. A Sharps would have gone right through, so somewhere in there is a bullet. And we have no idea how much damage it did.'

Dr Goodfellow uncorked the bottle of carbolic solution, thoroughly wet a cotton wad with it, and swabbed Stryker's entire abdomen. 'Now, Joseph, if you'll manage the chloroform, we'll see if we can repair the damage to this good man.'

Dr Craig covered Stryker's nose and mouth with a gauze

mask soaked in chloroform. 'Haven't done this since the war,' he muttered, 'but a man doesn't forget.'

Stryker's breathing deepened and slowed, and when his pulse slowed to about sixty per minute, Dr Craig said, 'He's under, George.'

'Good. Well then, let us begin.' Dr Goodfellow picked a scalpel from among the instruments on the commode. He dipped the scalpel in a bowl of carbolic acid solution. 'Persevere, Matthew Stryker, persevere,' he said. He inserted the scalpel into the bullet hole and split Stryker's belly almost to his navel.

12

Stryker woke with a terrible thirst, a stomach that threatened to upheave, and a pain that said he'd been slit from belly-button to breakfast. He groaned.

'That you, Matt?' Tom Hall's face appeared in Stryker's line of sight. The worry lines between his brows said he'd not slept for days.

Stryker groaned again. 'Shit fire,' he croaked. 'Feels like Buck Head Creek all over again.'

'You hang on, Matt. Just hang on.' Hall sidled toward the door, watching Stryker the whole time.

'I ain't dead, Tom. And ain't likely to be.'

'I'm gone.' Hall opened the door and slipped out. 'Doc. Doc! Hey, Doc.! Stryker's awake. Hey. Hey, Doc.'

Stryker heard Hall's shouts through the closed door. Any other day he might have chuckled. As it was, he moaned. For a little bitty bullet hole, he sure hurt in lots of places.

The door swung in. 'Well, well. You've come out from under the chloroform then. Splendid. I'll wager your stomach's a bit weak at this point. Can't let you have any solids right now anyway.'

'Hello to you, too, Doc,' Stryker croaked. It felt like the membranes of his throat cracked and tore whenever he spoke.

'Picked two-twenty grains of lead out of you, young man. Reckon that's nothing new to you, judging from the scars. Did surprisingly little damage, considering.'

The doctor turned to Theresa, who'd followed him into the room. 'Please see if you can find a teapot with a long spout. Let's see if we can get some moisture into Mr Stryker.'

'*Sí*, Señor Doctor,' she said. She bustled out and came barging back in before the doctor could continue his discourse.

'*Como esta?*' She held up a small china teapot with a prominent spout.

'That looks like Evangeline Craig's best pot,' the doctor said.

'*Sí.*'

The doctor filled the little teapot with water and held the spout to Stryker's lips. He was able to draw some into his mouth. It moistened the tissues. He felt like he was drinking from the spring at Tanner's Well after crossing forty miles of Mojave Desert. He closed his eyes and held the water in his mouth until it was nearly all soaked up by the dry tissues. He swallowed. A trickle ran down his throat. Bliss. He reached for the teapot.

'No you don't, Mr Stryker,' Dr Goodfellow said. 'You can have some more in a few minutes.'

'When do I get out of here?' Stryker's voice was no longer a croak.

'Listen to me, young man. I had to cut you from the bullet's entrance almost to your navel. That's a six-inch incision across the muscles of your abdomen. The bullet nicked your descending colon and your small intestine. Missed the spleen and kidneys. Lucky man, you are. Now, I've stitched your guts and cleaned all the shit out of your belly. I wiped it all down with carbolic solution, which should keep you from rotting away from the inside.'

'When can I get out of here,' Stryker asked again.

'I'd say two weeks.'

Stryker lay silent for a long moment. 'More water?' he said at last.

'Surely.'

This time he took two swallows before the doctor pulled the teapot away.

Tom Hall trailed Evangeline Craig into the sickroom. Once in the room, he stood back against the wall.

'Tom?' Stryker said.

'I'm here.'

'Talk.'

'No talk, young man, until you've eaten this,' Evangeline said.

Stryker eyed the portly woman. For a moment, he looked like he was going to revolt, but he only said, 'Yes, ma'am.'

'Your help, Mr Hall,' Evangeline said. 'And you, Dr Goodfellow. Theresa. Get ready with the pillows. Mr Hall, you over here. Doctor, you on this side. Ready? Now lift Mr Stryker so Theresa can put the pillows under him. There. Not sitting, but his head's up enough that he can eat.'

'Damn, but you're hard on a man,' Stryker said.

'Stop complaining. Eat.' She shoved a spoonful of goo into Stryker's open mouth.

'Yee gads,' he said after swallowing.

'Hardly gourmet fare, Mr Stryker, but rice gruel is best right now. Gives you strength without making stool.'

'Yes, ma'am,' he said, and passively ate a bowl full of half-liquid gruel.

When he was once more on his back, Stryker said, 'Tom. Tell me what's going on. Who pulled the trigger?'

'Tom Easter's working on that. Don't know much of anything yet.'

'How long've I been in here now?'

'Five days.'

'Damn gut hurts.'

'Man gets shot, he hurts.' Hall showed a little smile. 'Reckon you know that.'

'Where's St George?'

'Playing poker. Good place to hear things, he says.'

'Let me see your tongue, young man,' Dr Goodfellow said.

Stryker stuck out his tongue.

'Wider.' The doctor held Stryker's tongue down with a flat stick and peered inside his mouth. 'Good color. Your blood circulation must be doing well. Please call Dr Craig,' he said to Theresa.

'*Sí.*' Theresa bustled out, and moments later came back with Dr Craig in tow.

'You called, George?'

'This man Stryker has a constitution of a draft horse,' Dr Goodfellow said. 'He'll do well now, and be up in a few days.'

He looked down at Stryker. 'You, Matt Stryker, would do well to listen to what I say. Now, you know, Joseph, that I sutured the tears in this man's intestines with catgut. Those sutures will eventually dissolve and cause him no more problem. The fact that he's awake and cognizant says the irrigation of his abdominal sac was successful.'

'The incision is closed with silk, is it not?'

'Yes, and you can clip and remove the stitches in two weeks. Now. I'll return to Tucson on tomorrow's stage. If you run into complications, wire me. In the meantime, I'll be at the Palace. Must imbibe something refreshing.'

'Doc,' Stryker said. 'Thanks for putting me back together.'

'Men play with guns, they get shot,' Dr Goodfellow said. 'St George is a friend. You're his friend. We're on the same side, Stryker. One day we'll have a drink together. Right now, you're on gruel.'

'I didn't die from the bullet, so you're gonna starve me, then?'

A smile showed beneath Dr Goodfellow's moustache. 'You're on gruel until you pass a stool.'

'Stool?'

'Take a shit, in your vernacular,' the doctor said. 'Once you've passed a stool and there are no complications – you look for blood, red blood, in that stool, Joseph,' he said to Dr Craig. 'If there's none, feed him liver twice a day to build up his blood.'

'When can I get out of here?'

'After you've had a shit.'

'Shit.'

'That's what I said.'

Stryker scowled. 'I'll give it another day,' he said. 'I've got things to do.'

'Everyone leave the room,' Dr Goodfellow said. 'Rest is the best medicine. You've had a bowl of gruel. Now it's time for your morning nap. I'll drop in to see you before I return to Tucson.' The doctor herded everyone from the room and left Stryker staring at the ceiling.

'*Señor. Señor.*'

Stryker's eyes flew open. He was instantly awake and aware.

'*Señor. El mestizo esta aqui.*'

'*Mestizo?*'

'*Sí. Su nombre . . .*' She hesitated. '*Su nombre es Jake. El mestizo Jake.*'

'Injun Jake?'

'*Sí.*'

'So? Where is he?'

Theresa slipped from the room and returned with Injun Jake in tow.

110

'Help me sit,' Stryker said.

Theresa and Jake put a couple of pillows behind Stryker, then helped him get up so his back was against the wall.

'Better,' Stryker said. 'What is it?' he said to Jake.

'Tame Indians hear stuff. So do stable-muckers like Squirly and Wildman Kelly.'

'Good. Talk.'

'The woman ain't the only Powers in the game. Them Powerses is a whole army.'

Stryker said nothing, but his mind whirled. He had a job of work to do for Stan Ruggart. Melanie Powers hired Dumb Dickie to kill him in Rimrock.

'I reckon it were Dolbie James what pulled the trigger when you got shot,' Jake said.

'Mobeetie gunman?'

'That's him. Seems there's three James brothers what are cousins to Clayton Powers, whose sister is Melanie Powers. And whatever other guns they hire. They're talking about laying you out right here.'

Stryker searched his memory. 'That'll be Dolbie, Will Roy, and Rick James, then?'

'That's them. But Dolbie's the only one in town right now. His brothers is coming today sometime. Ain't seen them yet.'

'But they aim to get me here?'

'Dolbic met the girl as she were coming out of Ben Weaver's store. They talked where I could hear. Dolbie were upset that you ain't dead. Told the girl him and his brothers would take care of that tonight. I figure that meant here.' Jake leaned over and lowered his voice. 'You want us'uns to watch outside tonight?'

'Let's do something else,' Stryker said. 'Go find Dobie James, Jake. Tell him I want to talk to him. Tell him to bring his brothers and Melanie Powers, too. Or come by himself,

111

if that's what he wants.'

'You want him here? For sure?'

'I do.'

Injun Jake heaved a sigh. 'If that's what you want,' he said.

'One thing. Before you talk to Dolbie, could you get Ken St George to come over here?'

'Know where he is,' Jake said. 'I'll get him right away.'

'Thanks.'

Jake left, and Stryker said, 'Theresa.'

'*Sí*'

'Mr Hall, please.'

'*Sí.*'

Tom Hall burst into the room. 'You're sitting up,' he said.

'As you can see.'

'Shee-it.'

'Listen to me, Tom. Jake says Dolbie James is in town.'

'Mobeetie gunman?'

Stryker nodded. 'Jake says he likely pulled the trigger the other night.'

Hall's face clouded over. 'Want me to go get him?'

'If I'm not mistaken, he'll be here tonight. Maybe with Melanie Powers. Maybe by himself. But I reckon he'll come. Watch. Watch with Ken and Jake, but don't interfere.'

'So. How come you know he'll show up?'

'I asked him to come.'

'Shee-it.'

'You all be around. I want to see what he has to say for himself.'

Theresa barged into the room with a bowl of gruel. '*Se coma esto,*' she said.

Dolbie James came at midnight. He came alone, with a horn-handled Frontier Colt on his hip and a '73 Winchester .44-40 in his hand. No one made him leave his weapons

112

outside. No one said anything about what condition Matt Stryker might be in. And no one got in his way.

Theresa showed him to the sickroom.

Matt Stryker sat up in bed, back propped against the wall. 'Hello, Dolbie,' he said.

Dolbie James looked around the bare room. No place for gunmen to hide. He growled. 'I could blast you to hell,' he said.

Stryker nodded. 'You could. But you won't. I reckon that long shot the other night bothers you. I don't reckon you're the kind who likes to kill from ambush.'

'Weren't me.'

Stryker's eyebrows raised. 'Then maybe you'll listen to what I've got to say?'

Dolbie James looked around again, then scowled. 'Whacha wanna say?' he said.

'Farrell Roundy says you're straight on. Wild and easy to rile, but straight on—'

'You know Roundy?'

'We fought in the same war.'

Dolbie James said no more. He stood back against the wall and waited for Stryker to say his piece.

'So here I am, Dolbie. Gutshot but not dead, thanks to Dr Goodfellow. I came to Prescott to do a job I promised a dead man that I'd do. Now, as far as I can tell, Melanie Powers hired Dumb Dickie to kill me from ambush in Rimrock.'

'She never said nothing about Dumb Dickie.'

'Then when I got to Prescott, somebody shoots me before I can even get a night's rest in the Jeffery.'

'It weren't me.'

'I heard you, Dolbie. And I reckon you didn't, even though the doc cut a .44-40 slug from my guts.'

Dolbie James touched his gun like he was making sure it was in place.

'Two of my friends overheard Melanie talking to Dumb Dickie in the livery at Rimrock. Then I hear she's cousins with you and Will Roy and Rick. I hear you saying that night shot was a mistake that you're going to put right.'

Dolbie James nodded. 'You killed one of our kin. It weren't no lawman who cotch him. It were you, Matthew Stryker. It were just some common bounty hunter. You hunted Clayton down for money, and that ain't no better than Melanie paying Dumb Dickie to do you in.'

Stryker nodded like Dolbie had nodded. 'You've got a point, Dolbie. But I'd like to ask one favor of you.'

Dolbie James stood silent for a long moment. 'OK,' he said.

'You're a straight man, Dolbie. Mean as hell, but straight. Me? I can't even get out of bed. So, like I said, I've got something to do for a dead man. Something I promised, and you know, Dolbie, that a man's only as good as his word.'

'Get to it,' Dolbe James said, his voice edged like flint.

'You've got claim on me because of Clayton Powers. I'm no lawman, wasn't then anyway, but I brought Powers in belly down over his own saddle. You've got claim, Dolbie, and as soon as I've finished up what I promised to do, we can stand off, you and me, and I may die. Or you might die. But it will be straight, you and me, straight on. Can you do that?'

Dolbie James stood silent. 'OK,' he said. 'I'll do it. And so will my brothers. But I can't promise for Melanie. She fairly well does what she damn well pleases.'

'That's good enough for me, Dolbie. And thanks for coming.'

Dolbie James inspected the room one last time, then left.

Matt Stryker took the cocked Remington Army from under the sheets, let the hammer down, and set it on the side table. He blew out the lamp, squirmed around to where he could lie down full length, turned on his side, wrestled the pillow into a comfortable position, and went to sleep.

13

Two days on gruel and Stryker passed a stool. Dr Craig looked at the mess in the chamber pot and pronounced it free of new blood. 'You'll be up and around in no time,' he said.

As soon as the doctor left the sickroom, Stryker struggled to a sitting position with his legs hanging off the bed. Under the nightgown he was naked. A man doesn't like to be naked. He stood, but the stretching pain in his abdomen kept him skrinched over like an old woman. His clothes hung from pegs in the wall, but who knew where his union suit was? One hand on the wall, he gingerly walked to the chest of drawers across the room. His underwear was in the second drawer, along with his socks.

When Theresa came with fried liver and onions, Stryker sat in the room's only chair, fully clothed.

'*Señor, quedante in la cama*,' she said.

'Man heals quicker if he gets up and moves around,' Stryker said. 'Can I eat that sitting at a table?'

'*Aqui no hay ninguna mesa*,' Theresa said.

'Out there?' Stryker waved at the door.

Theresa thought for a moment, then set the food on the side table. She held a hand out to Stryker. '*Vamos*,' she said.

Stryker took her hand, which was exceptionally strong for

such a little woman. With a hand on her shoulder, he made his way to the dining-room table. He ate a plateful of fried liver and onions along with a healthy serving of fried potatoes, then walked back to the sickroom on his own. 'Best a man get moving, if he wants a wound to heal,' he said.

He sat in the straight-back chair when Tom Hall returned.

'You up?' Hall said.

'What's it look like? Time to go back to the Jeffery. How far is it?'

'Walking or riding?'

'Reckon I'd better walk. Man needs to stand on his own two feet when he's been shot.'

'Good enough. When.'

'No time like right now,' Stryker said. 'Could you get the doc?'

'Sure.' Hall left.

Stryker got his gun rig off the wall. But he rolled it up and buckled the belt around it rather than putting it on.

'What's this about leaving?' Dr Craig said on his way in.

'Time to leave, Doc. What do I owe you?'

Dr Craig scratched his Lincolnesque beard. 'Let's see. Seven dollars for the week you've been here, three dollars for medicine and so forth, and three fifty for meals. Adds up to thirteen fifty, all told.'

'What about Doc Goodfellow?'

'He said he owed a favor to Kensington St George. Said to drop by some time when you're in Tucson and buy him a drink or two.'

'I reckon I owe that man.'

Dr Craig smiled and gave a short nod. 'That you do. Not many doctors in this country can do what he does with gunshot wounds. Best I've ever seen.' The doctor's face went somber. 'Wish we'd known in '64 what George Goodfellow's showed us now. Lots more young men would be alive instead

117

of lying in shallow graves at Bloody Tank and Antietam and Cold Mountain.' He sighed.

Stryker dug two eagles from his vest pocket. 'This should cover what I owe,' he said. 'And give Theresa a little extra, if you please.'

Dr Craig took the eagles with a grin. 'She'll appreciate that,' he said. 'Her with four youngsters to provide for.'

'Good. Tom. Let's meander on over to the Jeffery,' Stryker said. He handed Hall the rolled-up gun rig. 'Carry that, can you?'

Hall raised an eyebrow, but said nothing. He accepted the holstered Remington and stretched out a hand to help Stryker to his feet. 'We're off,' he said.

On a sunny day, the walk from Dr Craig's house to the Jeffery would take ten minutes, less on a horse. Stryker and Hall made it in just under half an hour.

Kensington St George sat in the lobby reading the *Arizona Democrat* when they walked in. 'Looks like Doc Goodfellow didn't chop you in half,' he said. 'He can get careless when he's had too much liquor, and that man does like his liquor.'

'Hello to you, too, Ken,' Stryker said.

'Town's getting crowded,' St George said.

'New capital of the territory. That ain't surprising.'

'You know about the Powers woman and her kin, I reckon, but there are more.'

'Like who?'

'Like Elizabeth Wharton and her gambling man, Virgil Teague.'

'Stan's used-to-be wife. The vultures gather.'

'They do. Supper?'

'Ate at Doc Craig's. They've got me on liver for my blood. Wouldn't mind some good coffee though.'

'Scully's got decent coffee, and it's right here at the Jeffery.'

'Lead on. Coming, Tom?'

'Be there directly,' Hall said. 'You want this?' He held up the holstered Remington.

'Not in shape to fight with guns right now. Let's give it a day or two. Whoever shoots me will have to put a bullet in an unarmed man.'

'You think they won't?'

'They might. But I've been shot before. Ain't dead yet.'

Hall snorted. 'Damn near, though.'

'Thanks, Tom. See you at Scully's.'

Hall got the keys to 213 and 214 and climbed the stairs. Stryker and St George went out and around the corner of the hotel to Scully's. St George ordered a steak with trimmings and coffee, Stryker coffee only.

The restaurant had lamps on the walls that threw a soft yellow light on the big square room. Four rows of four tables, most occupied by men. Stryker's eyes passed over the two ranch wives who sat with their husbands against the far wall. Miners sat at four of the tables and several others were full of politicians and their hangers-on. His eye stopped at a table occupied by a single woman. The moment he saw her, he understood what the term 'rare beauty' really meant. She seemed absorbed in her own thoughts. Her dark hair was pulled into a tight chignon and a small velvet-covered hat with a feathery plume clung to the top of her head. Lace frilled at her wrists, and the dark plum of her dress was accented with brocade. A single gold medallion hung from a yellow ribbon that encircled the high neck of her dress. Puffed sleeves seemed to broaden her shoulders while her waist looked impossibly tiny. The gold of her dangling earrings matched he medallion. Her creamy complexion was without makeup, her eyebrows were black and sharp, and her eyelashes accented the deep blue of her irises.

Stryker realized he was staring, and quickly turned his

119

eyes away. When he glanced back at her, she was smiling.

'Catherine is a gorgeous woman,' St George said.

'The one sitting alone? Absolutely. Understatement if anything.'

St George stood and walked over to Catherine de Merode's table. He said something to her and indicated Stryker's table with one hand. Catherine nodded. St George pulled back her chair as she rose, then escorted her to the seat at Stryker's left. 'Miss de Merode accepted my invitation to join us, Matt,' he said.

Stryker struggled to his feet and removed his hat. 'Matthew Stryker, ma'am. Pleased.'

Catherine curtsied. 'A pleasure, Marshal. This will save me the bother of looking you up.' She sat, moving as gracefully as any French ballerina.

'Thank you, ma'am. But why would you do something like that? Look me up, that is.'

'Rodham McKendrick, the man who hired me, has been informed that the part owner of the Dominion mine, Stanford Ruggart, is dead. Furthermore, you, Marshal Matthew Stryker, seem to hold papers that may determine how Mr Ruggart's holdings are to be handled. In a legal sense, of course.'

'Yes, ma'am, that is true, as far as it goes. Do you represent Mr McKendrick?'

'Oh my, no. He hired me to be interim governess to Mr Ruggart's daughter, April. She should arrive in Prescott shortly.

'You let that girl travel from San Francisco by herself?'

'No, of course not. Mr McKendrick hired the Pinkerton Agency to provide an escort for her. I believe the man's name is Lou Grimes.'

'Shotgun Lou Grimes?'

'Perhaps. He has a reputation as a rough character, I hear,

but Pinkerton's Denver chief of staff vouched for his honesty.'

'Shee-it.'

'Sir?'

'Nothing. One more iron in the fire,' Stryker said.

St George and Catherine fell into conversation about a stage show they'd seen in San Francisco. Stryker sipped his coffee and brooded about Stan Ruggart's will.

Tom Hall joined them. He ordered a steak to match St George's, and he couldn't keep his eyes off Catherine de Merode. She, on the other hand, often glanced at Matt Stryker.

Stryker felt better in the morning. He could stand without having to skrinch over to ease the stretch at the scar across his belly. The hotel had sponged off his coat and hat, and he had a new shirt from Weaver's general store. Someone had even blacked his boots. He locked his door on the way out and rapped on 214. 'Tom Hall. Sun's been up for an hour or so. Time to get some breakfast.'

The clerk's head showed at the top of the stairs. 'Mr Hall has gone out, sir,' he called. 'He asked me to tell you to wait for him at the Old Mill on Gurley. Be there shortly, he said.'

'Thanks, son,' Stryker said. He thought for a moment about going back for his Remington, but decided against it. Prescott was the capital of the Arizona Territory, civilized. The war had been over for nearly fifteen years. Ordinary folks were replacing the loners who came in with Whipple and Sitgreaves and Bill Williams. On the other hand, Isaiah Parker and Judge Roy Bean came down hard on the outlaws in the Indian Nations and in West Texas, so lawless men drifted into New Mexico and Arizona, holing up in Mexican Hat, Big Johney Gulch, Alma, and Round Valley. But that was there, and this was here, in the shadow of the capitol

121

building, the courts of Arizona and Yavapai County. And
Tom Easter wore the marshal's badge. So even though he'd
been shot from the dark, Matt Stryker went to breakfast
without a gun.

The early-morning breakfast crowd was gone and the late
eaters had yet to arrive. Matt Stryker took a table that put his
back to a wall and the windows on the street at his right
hand. He hung his hat on a tree in the corner.

'I'm Julie,' the waitress said. 'Having breakfast?'

'You cooking?'

She laughed. 'You don't want no breakfast I cook. I can't
even boil water without it getting scorched. But Snuffy works
magic back there in the kitchen.'

'Snuffy Duggan?'

'Why yes. Do you know him?'

'I ate more of his beef and beans than I ever want to
admit. All the way from Fort Worth to Abilene. Tell him Matt
Stryker's here and needs some liver and three eggs over easy,
and a few fried potatoes, too.'

'Abilene, eh? I'll tell him. Coffee?'

'Right now'd be soon enough.'

A young woman at the table opposite Stryker's looked up
sharply when he said his name. Moments later, she left,
more than half her breakfast uneaten on her plate.

Stryker saw her, but thought little of her quick departure.

'Matt Stryker, you old bulldogger. How in hell are ya
anyway?'

'Hello, Snuffy. Never figured you for a downtown cook.
You're made for Dutch ovens and two-gallon coffee pots by
a good oak fire.'

'I know that, Matt, but a man's gotta eat and the railroads
killed the big cattle drives. I'll get me a plush job at some
ranch one of these days. Anyway, liver? You been shot?'

'I have. Funny you've not heard of it. Need liver to build

up my blood, the doc says. You got any?'

'Man, we run though two-year-old beeves like they're going out of style. Got a liver from yesterday. What'll yah gave? Three slices? Four?'

'Three's fine, Snuffy. Good to eat your slop again, old woman.'

The cook laughed at Stryker's trail drive lingo. 'Old woman I may be, but at least you can eat what I fix. Some ain't fit for human beens and you know it. Liver coming up.' He disappeared into the kitchen.

Julie brought a cup and filled it from a two-quart coffee pot. 'That's to hold you until the liver's done,' she said.

Stryker nodded, smiling at the thought of Snuffy Duggan's coffee. Black as the insides of the Devil himself, and strong as a bull buffalo. He took a sip and let out a sigh. Nothing had changed. The taste of the brew took Stryker back to the days right after the war when chousing a herd north over the Chisum Trail was about the only way a Texan who'd fought for the South could make a living. A hard life, but a life. He took another sip. Damn. What a good cup of coffee couldn't do for a man.

No mistaking the double click of shotgun hammers being eared back. Stryker reacted without conscious thought. He dropped from the chair, putting his bodyweight on the edge of the table to tip it up on its side. The underside of the table took the buckshot fired from across the room. Three steps closer and the shot would have gone through.

'Throw it down,' Snuffy Duggan shouted from the kitchen doorway. 'I wouldn't want to blow you all to hell, miss, but you just put that scattergun on the floor. Gently now. Easy. Just put it down. That's a good girl. You can come out from behind that table now, Matt.'

Stryker struggled to his feet. The three-day-old wound Dr Goodfellow made with his scalpel hurt like fire. He just hoped nothing inside had come apart.

Snuffy Duggan stood spraddle-legged in the doorway, an ancient Dragoon Colt in his hand. The young woman who'd rushed from the restaurant was just inside the front door. A double-barrelled Greener lay on the floor in front of her. Tears streamed down her cheeks but her face was filled with determination, and hate.

'You!' she screamed. 'You!'

She put her face in her hands and turned to the wall. Her shoulders heaved and great sobs shook her body. She threw back her head and howled, sounding more animal than human. She turned to face Stryker again, sobbing. She pointed at him, her arm straight as a spear, her index finger an accusing point. 'You.' She sniffled. 'Killed.' Hiccup. 'My.' Another sniffle. 'BROTHER!' She broke down again. 'Dear God. Dear God, what can I do? My brother's gone and this merciless killer who murdered him lives. It is not fair, God. Not. Fair.'

Stryker sat down, hand on the sutured incision beneath the swath of muslin around his abdomen. 'Good Lord, lady,' he said. 'At least you could let a man eat his breakfast.'

Tom Hall burst through the door, a long 3-barrel Baker 10-gauge in his hands. 'Matt!'

'All right, Tom. If the stitches held. Don't hurt quite so much now.'

Hall picked the Greener up, broke it open, and pulled out the spent shells, holding the Baker in the crook of his left arm. 'Miss,' he said, 'you've been trying to kill my friend Matt Stryker since you sicced Dumb Dickie on him in Rimrock. I reckon you or one of yours shot him from the dark across Montezuma the other night.'

He tapped the woman on the shoulder. 'Look at me, lady,' he said.

She lifted her tear-streaked face.

'Matt Stryker killed Clayton Powers. That's no lie. But let me tell you this. I know Matt Stryker. A straighter man never lived. And I'll tell you another thing. When Clayton Powers died, he had a gun in his hand and he faced Matt Stryker head on. Matt didn't shoot him in the back and Matt didn't pull his trigger first. He's not that kind of man.'

The woman stared at the floor.

'Look at me!' Hall said in a flint-hard voice.

She complied.

'Clayton Powers had a price on his head, miss. He shot and killed a US marshal in Las Cruces. He was wanted, dead or alive. If he could've, Matt would've brought Powers in alive. Then your brother would have hanged. I reckon he came at Matt Stryker the way he did because he wanted to die quick of a bullet rather than slow and painful, kicking at the end of a rope.'

Hall shoved the Greener out. 'Take your gun, miss. But don't you point it at Matt Stryker again.'

She took a long look at Tom Hall's hard face, grabbed the Greener, and fled.

14

The table's underside was peppered with shot, but wasn't damaged structurally. Set upright, it showed nothing of its encounter with Melanie Powers's shotgun.

'Matt Stryker, I'm starting to think you draw gunfire like a dead mule draws flies,' Tom Hall said.

'What's with the cannon?' Stryker asked.

'Went and got me a good Baker 10-guage 3-barrel, .44-40 for good measure,' Hall said. 'I reckon any shooting's going to be close up and it's real hard to miss with a shotgun at anything less than about forty feet. Should help me watch your back a little better.'

'That girl like to shot me,' Stryker said. 'Man can move fast when a shotgun's pointed at him, cut belly or no.'

Julie picked up the silverware from the floor and brought new settings. 'How 'bout you, mister,' she said to Tom Hall.

'Sow belly with two eggs and a man-size hunk of sourdough,' Hall said.

'You got it. Fried liver coming right up, Mr Stryker.'

Julie disappeared into the kitchen just as Tom Easter came in the front door. He strode to Matt Stryker's table and stood there for a moment, looking down at him. 'There's been more gunfire since you rode into town than I've seen all month.' Easter's face was hard. 'Think it's gonna let up?'

'No way of telling, Tom. You know I can't promise anything other than none of it will be started by me.'

Easter heaved a sigh. 'Sure wish you'd get your business done and get on outta my town.'

Stryker took a long look at Tom Easter's face, and he saw no give in it. No hint of mirth, no indication that Easter was on his side. 'Reckon I'd feel the same way in your shoes,' he said.

Easter nodded. 'I'll have a word with that woman,' he said. He paused. 'Take care, Matt. I'd hate to have to bury you here. You might want to know that the Yavapai county sheriff is in town. Dan O'Mara. Politician, he is, but he's a straight man, too. He may be wanting to talk to you about Rimrock. What do you think of taking some time off, going to Tucson or San Francisco or somewhere until things settle down?'

Stryker took a sip of his coffee, lukewarm. He studied on what he had to say, then said it. 'Tom, a man died in my town. He was harmless, a drunk, but straight as the day is long and never a bother to anybody. Someone killed him, and he knew it was coming. He asked me to find the killer before he even died. And he asked me after he was dead.'

'After?'

Stryker nodded. 'After. He left an envelope with me to be opened if he got killed. I don't know if he was a friend, but he was a citizen of Rimrock and it was my job to keep him from getting killed. Dead, he asked me to do some other things for him, Tom, and that's why I'm here in Prescott. I can't leave until the job's done.'

Julie came from the kitchen with big stoneware plates heaped with breakfast. 'Gentlemen,' she said. 'Courtesy of Snuffy Duggan.' She set the plates down. 'Be right back with more coffee.'

She hustled back to the kitchen and returned with the

two-quart coffee pot. Tom Easter lifted a hand to Stryker and Hall. 'I hear you, Matt, but I still don't want to have to bury you.' He left.

Matt Stryker ate stolidly, stabbing pieces of liver as if they were enemies. Tom Hall glanced at him now and again as they cleared their plates of Snuffy Duggan's good chow.

Gradually, the Old Mill filled up and the room buzzed with babble. Matt Stryker shovelled in a last forkful of fried potatoes dripping with egg yolk and washed it down with a gulp of coffee. He hardly even chewed.

'Time to get ready to go see the judge,' he said. He pushed back his chair and stood to go. He retrieved his black Stetson from the tree and clamped it securely on his head. 'Damn place where Doc Goodfellow sliced into me hurts like hell,' he said. 'Let's go.'

'You'd better pay for the meal,' Tom Hall said.

'Julie! What do we owe you?'

Julie came bustling over after she delivered an armload of Snuffy Duggan's food to a nearby table. 'Four bits for the two of you,' she said.

'You got change?' he asked Tom Hall.

'Yeah.' Hall dug coins from his trousers, picked out two quarters, and handed them to Julie. 'Thanks for the good grub,' he said.

'Welcome, Tom. Matt. Come again sometime when women with shotguns ain't chasing you.' She smiled.

'Yes, ma'am.' Stryker put a forefinger to the brim of his hat. 'We will be back ... at least I will ... without the shotgun. Come on, Tom.' He headed for the door.

'Leaving without a word, then?' Snuffy Duggan said from the kitchen when Stryker and Hall walked by.

'Figured you were busy at the stove, old woman,' Stryker said. 'Besides, we'll be back.'

'Take care, Matt. Someone don't like you atall.'

Stryker noticed the handle of Snuffy's Dragoon sticking out above his apron. 'I'll try to be careful, Snuffy. My every intention is completely peaceful.'

'Where to?' Hall asked as they left.

'Back to the Jeffery to pick up some papers, then across to the courthouse. Got to be a judge in there somewhere.'

'OK.' Hall shifted the Baker to the crook of his left arm and walked a half-step behind Stryker. His eyes had the restless look of a cougar caught in a tight place. He didn't say another word until they reached the Jeffery. Injun Jake sat hunkered down near the hotel entrance.

Injun Jake stood up. 'Marshal,' he said.

'People in this town gunning for me, Jake.'

'I'm watching, Marshal, but I can't be everywhere all at once. There ain't no one in the hotel as I can tell. But a man never knows.'

Under his floppy hat, faded cast-off cavalry shirt and old canvas trousers, Jake looked like any other tame Indian on the streets, except for his eyes. Jacob Bent had eyes that never missed a thing.

'I feel better with you watching, Jake,' Stryker said.

Tom Hall went into the Jeffery first, the Baker 10-gauge slanted casually in his hands, but ready for instant use.

Stryker followed two steps behind.

'Marshal Stryker?' Catherine de Merode's melodious voice sounded across the lobby. She sat in the far corner where a divan and two armchairs surrounded a low table. A young girl and a short-coupled man with a coach gun sat with her.

Tom Hall stepped between Stryker and Catherine.

'What is it, Mr Hall?' Catherine said.

'My friend got shot at once this morning,' Hall said. 'Don't want that to happen again. Who's your friend with the coach gun?'

129

Catherine laughed. 'Oh my, Mr Hall. We of all people do not wish to see Matthew Stryker dead.' She held her hand out to the girl. 'Come, April,' she said.

The girl stood, and Stryker could see Stan Ruggart in the light brown of her hair and the slant of her eyes, in the shape of her nose and the single dimple on her right cheek. 'April Ruggart?'

'Yes, sir,' she said.

'Then you'll be Shotgun Lou Grimes,' Stryker said, looking at the man with the coach gun.

'I am.'

'Thank you for seeing April safe to Prescott.'

Grimes nodded.

'Could you stay on a few more days?'

'Ten dollars a day,' Grimes said. 'Who's paying?'

'I'll see that you get paid, Grimes,' Stryker said. 'Could you get together with Tom Hall here and talk about things?'

'Tom Hall?'

'This here's Tom Hall.'

'Tom Hall from El Paso way?'

'The same,' Hall said.

'Well, Marshal. When you get help, you get the best,' Grimes said. 'Pleased to know you, Tom Hall.' He made no move to shake hands.

'I got Matt's back, Lou Grimes. You take care of the little girl,' Hall said.

'I'll do what the Marshal asks,' Grimes said. 'He foots the bill.'

To Whom It May Concern:
The Last Will and Testament of Stanford Jameson Ruggart is to be read in public and probated in the chambers of the Honorable Leland B. Westover, Chief Justice, Territory of Arizona, promptly at 9 a.m. on July

130

11, 1879. All with an interest in the proceedings shall be seated in the chambers prior to that time.

Signed:

Martin Hayes

Clerk to the Court

The Arizona capitol building and courthouse stood back from Montezuma Street, across from the saloons on Whiskey Row. Matt Stryker had been in courthouses before, but mostly he administered the law with the barrel of a good Remington Army .44, mostly without pulling the trigger, and mostly without injuring anyone much.

He sat in the front row of the pewlike benches. The room sobered anyone who entered. Walls panelled waist-high with mahogany. The judge's seat set a good three feet higher than the rest of the room. Dark-red velvet draperies hid the door the judge would enter through. An American flag stood on a flagpole to the right of the judge's seat, its field showing thirty-eight stars. Large paintings of George Washington and Thomas Jefferson on one wall, a photograph of John Fremont, the pathfinder and current – though absentee – governor of Arizona on another. Stryker resisted an urge to scratch the itchy scar on his abdomen.

A number of people sat in the room, perhaps because of the public announcement. Stryker knew some and surmised over others. Injun Jake, who carried a long thin knife in one boot, was two rows back, Tom Hall another row behind Jake. Catherine de Merode and April Ruggart sat beside Stryker. Kensington St George lounged in the row across from Tom Hall.

April tugged on Stryker's sleeve. He leaned down. 'That's my mother,' she whispered, nodding toward a woman in a dark dress and hat with a black veil. A tall courtly man with long slim fingers accompanied her.

131

The doors at the back of the room swung open and a large well-dressed man walked in, followed by a thin bespectacled gentleman in a dove-gray suit and tight bowler. The big man doffed his short-brimmed hat as he entered and strode down the center aisle to take a seat just behind Stryker. The small man sat beside him.

'Matthew Stryker?' the big man said.

Stryker turned. 'Yes?'

'I am Rodham Mckendrick,' he said. 'The gentleman at my side is Josiah Fish, who has managed Stan Ruggart's financial affairs for some years.

'Pleasure,' Stryker said.

'All stand,' called the clerk.

Everyone stood while Judge Westover entered the courtroom and took his seat behind the bench. At a scuffle of sound in the back, Stryker turned his head far enough to catch Squirly and Wildman Kelly slipping in and sitting next to Injun Jake.

'Be seated.'

From beneath bushy gray eyebrows Judge Westover stared at the people who waited for probate of Stanford Ruggart's last will and testimony. He waved a hand at the clerk. 'State the court's business,' he said.

The clerk stood and droned. 'The court is convened on this day, July the eleventh of eighteen and seventy-nine to probate the last will and testimony of the late Stanford Jameson Ruggart, then-resident of Rimrock, Yavapai County, Territory of Arizona. Judge Leland B. Westover, presiding.'

'Hey Judge.' Lizzimae stood up. 'Hey Judge,' she repeated. 'I'm Stan Ruggart's wife. My name is Elizabeth Ruggart. Whatever he's got is mine. Ain't that what the law says?'

The judge said nothing for a long moment, his eyes fastened on Lizzimae. She lifted her chin and met his stare without dropping her gaze, but Stryker noticed white knuckles on the hand that grasped the back of the bench in front of her. She wasn't as confident as her brazen voice would have people think.

'The writ,' Judge Westover said.

The clerk leafed through the papers on his desk, selected one, and handed it to the judge.

Judge Westover cleared his throat and held the writ at nearly arm's length. Still, he squinted. 'According to this document,' he said, 'Stanford Jameson Ruggart was granted a divorce from Elizabeth Mae Ruggart née Wharton on grounds of desertion. The writ is dated March the seventeenth of eighteen hundred and seventy nine. It is signed by Adolfus Livingston Witherspoon, Circuit Justice, County of Yavapai, Territory of Arizona.'

He returned the writ to the clerk and skewered Lizzimae with a glare. 'As you heard, Miss Wharton, the late Stanford Ruggart filed for and received divorce from you more than four months ago. Now, you may sit and listen to Mr Ruggart's last will and testament, or you may leave.' Judge Westover picked up his gavel and struck the block.

Lizzimae sobbed, then fled the room. The man who'd sat beside her stayed.

The judge's eyes bored into each person in the room. Silence. He held his hand out to the clerk. 'The will,' he said.

The clerk dutifully turned three sheets of paper over to Judge Westover. The judge flattened the will out on his bench, again at arm's length, squinted at it, and began to read.

133

15

'Last Will and Testament of Stanford Jameson Ruggart

"I, Stanford Jamerson Ruggart, residing at Room 7 of the Rimrock Hotel, in Rimrock, Arizona, declare that this is my last will and testament and that there is no other.

"First: I declare that I am not married. At the same time, I declare that I have one daughter, April Veronica Ruggart, who currently resides in San Francisco, California."

April nudged Stryker. 'That's me,' she whispered.

"Second: I nominate and appoint Matthew Bancroft Stryker as my personal representative in matters concerning and laid out by this last well and testament. When and if he is unable to continue as my representative, he shall designate a person to assume the responsibility.

"The personal representative will have full discretionary power to take any action desirable for administration of my estate, which means he can buy or sell anything under my name and he can distribute whatever is left of my estate as he sees fit.

"My estate shall pay the sum of one thousand dollars monthly into an account specified by Matthew Stryker, as long as he acts as my personal representative.

"Third: I direct that all fees, expenses, and taxes associated with my death be paid from whatever monies have accrued in my account at Wells Fargo Bank in Prescott, Arizona.

"Fourth: Elizabeth Mae Wharton shall receive one-third of the cash funds residing in the care of Mr Josiah Fish, who handles my investments and finances. She shall also receive one-third of the monies in my account at Wells Fargo Bank in Prescott, Arizona. My personal representative shall see that this provision is executed. However, if Elizabeth Mae Wharton is proven to have had any involvement, direct or indirect, with my death, this bequeathment shall be null and void." '

Stan knew it was coming. Stryker hadn't thought of Lizzimae as the one back of Ruggart's death, but Ruggart himself seemed to think she might have something to do with it. Stryker decided to look into her.

"The remainder of my estate shall be put in trust for April Veronica Ruggart until such time as she reaches her majority. Furthermore, this estate shall ever be her possession and never devolve upon another entity regardless of her marital status. She may, however, appoint whom she will to manage said estate." '

Again, Judge Westover lifted his eyes to survey the people in the courtroom. 'With your permission, Mr Stryker, we'll determine just what Mr Ruggart's estate consists of. Does that meet with your approval?'

Stryker stood. 'Certainly, Your Honor.'

'Mr Fish. Do I understand correctly that you are in charge of the finances of Stanford Ruggart?' the judge asked.

The little man in the gray suit stood. 'Yes, Your Honor.'

'And can you give us an idea of the worth of Mr Ruggart's estate?'

'Five million, one hundred seventy-three thousand fifty-three dollars and sixty-four cents, Your Honor, in properties, securities, investments, and cash as of closure of the books at six o'clock last evening. The figure includes both real estate and securities at the prices paid for them.'

The room was silent as a tomb. Then a rustle of paper as Fish removed a packet from his worn leather case. 'The exact particulars are in this report,' he said. 'If it please the court.'

Judge Westover held out a meaty hand.

Fish sidled to the aisle, opened the docket gate, and strode to the bench. He stood on tiptoe to hand the thin sheaf of papers to the judge.

'Thank you, Mr Fish. As personal representative, Mr Stryker now has control of these assets. Is that clear?'

'Yes, Your Honor.'

'A moment.' He turned toward the clerk. 'Swear Mr Fish in,' he said.

The clerk stood. 'Raise your right hand, please,' he said. 'Do you swear to tell the whole truth and nothing but the truth so help you God?'

'I do,' Fish said.

'Does this document represent the entire estate of Stanford Jameson Ruggart, deceased, Mr Fish?'

'All of which I was given custody, Your Honor.'

'Then affix your signature to the end of the document and add today's date,' the judge said.

'Yes, Your Honor.' Fish took a quill, dipped it in the inkpot, signed the final page of his report, then added the date. The clerk sanded the signature and returned the document to Judge Westover.

Teague found Lizzimae on the bed in their room at the Stanton Hotel. Apparently she'd cried herself to sleep. Now she lay with her mouth half open, and her cheek streaked with the remains of the kohl she used to line her eyes. He shook her shoulder.

'Go 'way.'

He shook her again, harder. 'Wake up, you stupid bitch.'

'Wha—? Who?' Lizzimae mumbled. Her eyes opened part-way. 'Oh. You. Leave me alone. He divorced me. The bastard. The stupid crazy drunken bastard.'

Teague slapped her face. 'Wake up, bitch,' he said through clenched teeth.

Lizzimae sat up, her hand on her flaming cheek. 'You hit me.'

'I'll beat you to within an inch of your life if you don't get some sense into that silly head of yours.'

'You. Hit. Me.'

Teague backhanded her.

She yowled.

'Sit up and listen, bitch.' Not a hint of softness in Teague's words. 'If you'd not run out of the courtroom, you wouldn't be crying,' he said. 'Ruggart left one-third of his money to you, bitch. One third.'

Lizzimae sat in silence. Blood oozed from a split in her lip and leaked from one nostril. 'One third?' she said. 'How much is one third?'

'His assets are worth more than five million,' Teague said.

Lizzimae sat up straight, her bruises forgotten. 'Five million? How much is mine?'

137

'Who knows? One third of "cash funds", the judge said. Whatever, it's a haul.'

Lizzimae pouted. 'I want the mine. I want everything that drunk had. Sumbitch.'

Teague sighed. 'Take what you can, Lizzimae. Make trouble and we'll lose it all.'

'What I do, people don't have to know,' she said.

'Well, right now, you've got more money than you ever dreamed of, I'd say. Just let it be.'

In the silence, the faint shouts of a teamster came from the street outside. A wagon clattered by. 'Let it be, Lizzimae,' Teague said again. 'That man Stryker was appointed Ruggart's personal representative. He'll be giving out the money. We still owe Barber Orv fifteen hundred.'

Lizzimae sniffed. 'I must look a mess. A bath and a different dress. I must look like a woman of means now,' she said. 'Let me get cleaned up. Then we can go see this Stryker fellow.' She gave Teague a coy smile, bloody mouth and nose not withstanding. 'Wanna fuck?'

He cast his eyes at the ceiling.

'Then be a good partner and get the hotel people to set up my bath in here,' she said.

Teague left without a word. He had things to think about, things to do, things more important than watching Lizzimae bathe, although he had to admit he'd be hard-pressed to come up with a woman that looked better in the bath than Lizzimae.

Matt Stryker, Rod McKendrick, Catherine de Merode, and April Ruggart filled Josiah Fish's small Prescott office to overflowing. He'd borrowed a chair from next door for April. She and Catherine sat to one side while Stryker and McKendrick faced Fish across his immaculate desk.

'As of the end of stock trading yesterday, at which I

138

ordered my broker to sell Mr Ruggart's holdings in Union Pacific Railway stocks, the balance in his various bank accounts equalled . . .' He referred to a yellow telegram and added a figure to the sheet of paper on his desk. '. . . Two million nine hundred and thirty-four thousand two hundred seventeen dollars and twenty-six cents.'

'Basically three million, then,' Stryker said. 'Please make out a bank draft for one million for Lizzimae . . . if she pans out.'

'Surely,' Fish said.

McKendrick turned to Stryker. 'Matt, I've got a buyer for the Dominion. I think Stan's shares should be part of the deal. What do you say?'

Stryker looked at Fish, his eyebrows raised.

'I suggest doing as Mr McKendrick says,' Fish said.

'Done,' Stryker said. 'The proceeds from the sale of Dominion shares, then, will go to Mr Fish.'

'Please. I'm Josiah.'

'OK. Josiah.' Stryker fell silent, his arms folded, his chin on his chest.

Fish broke the silence. 'Any more instructions, Mr Stryker?'

Stryker started. Then looked sheepishly from face to face. 'I've never done this before,' he said. 'There's a lot to think about.'

He turned to April and Catherine. 'And I've never had children, either.'

April's eyes sparkled. 'Are you going to be my daddy, sir?'

Stryker couldn't answer. The girl's mother had deserted her. Her father had been a drunk, though not a violent one. She'd had precious little experience with adults who cared for her. What kind of woman would she become? Would she have the judgment to sift the silver from the dross? God. What a job Stan Ruggart had shoved on to his shoulders. He sighed, and gave April a weak smile.

'April, I'm not your daddy. But you can write this on your heart. "Matt Stryker is my friend. I can always trust him". OK?'

April gave a short nod. 'I'll remember.' She paused a long moment. Then in a very small voice, she said, 'Could I call you Uncle Matt?'

16

After Catherine and April went to their rooms Stryker and Tom Hall decided to walk to the Palace for a drink or two. Stryker strapped on his Remington for the first time since Doc Goodfellow cut him open. Tom Hall carried his Baker. As they turned toward Montezuma Street, Injun Jake spoke from the shadows. 'Marshal. Heard something mighty strange today.'

Stryker and Hall slowed.

'They's a barber further up on Gurley,' Jake said. 'Claims his name is Harry Thompson. That gambler Virg Teague, well, he went to see that barber, and called him Orv.'

'Barber Orv?'

'Only Orv. Said he owed the barber fifteen hundred bucks.'

'Barber Orv.' Stryker remembered the flyer on his desk in Rimrock. 'Hmmm. Thank you, Jake.'

Stryker and Hall walked side by side. One tall and broad, the other shorter and wiry. Jake Bent slouched along several steps behind, a tame Indian who just happened to be going in the same direction.

'Stan Ruggart had his throat cut,' Hall said, his voice just loud enough for Stryker to hear.

Stryker nodded. 'I saw him.'

141

They went through the door to the Palace and gave their guns to Kincaid.

'Enjoy yourselves, gentlemen,' Kincaid said. 'Sorry to hear about the mishap when you last dropped in.' He disappeared into the cloakroom.

Tom Easter sat at the table farthest from the door, his back to the wall and a beer in front of him. Stryker raised a hand in greeting and Easter waved him over. 'Get me a beer, would you, Tom? I'll be at Marshal Easter's table.'

Hall went to the bar while Stryker walked on toward Easter's table. The Palace was as fancy as a place could be, but it still smelled of stale beer, tobacco juice that missed the spittoons, and old cigar smoke.

'Tom,' Stryker said.

'Sit?'

'Obliged. Tom Hall's getting me a beer.'

'You can drink beer with a bullet in your guts?'

'Seems all right.' Stryker paused a moment. 'Tom, you checked out that barber up on Gurley Street?'

'Just opened up. Harry Thompson, right?'

'I reckon he may be Barber Orv.'

'Barber Orv? Orvil Randall? What makes you figure that?'

'Trust me on this one, Tom. Take a close look.'

Tom Hall came over with a tall glass of beer in one hand and a bottle of Old Grand-Dad and a shot glass in the other. He sat in the chair to Easter's right, turning it slightly to face the center of the barroom. 'We got company,' Hall said. He indicated three newcomers with his chin.

'God,' Stryker said. 'Why can't they leave well-enough alone?'

Easter pushed his coat tail back behind the butt of his Peacemaker.

The three men stopped a good ten feet from the table.

'Now's not the time, James,' Stryker said.

'Do I look ready for a gunfight?' Dolbie James said. 'Damn Mick took our guns. Wouldn't let us in with 'em.'

'Smart man, Kincaid,' Easter said.

'So if it's not a gunfight, then what?' Stryker said.

'Oh, it's a gunfight, Stryker. You killed one of us. A blood relative. If you can't rely on blood relatives, there ain't much left.'

'I told you, Dolbie James, Clayton Powers could have surrendered and let the law take care of things.'

'You're a goldam bounty hunter, Stryker. You ain't got a badge. You ain't got no right to haul people in just because someone's willing to pay some cash for a dead body.'

James took a step toward the table and Tom Easter put a hand to the butt of his Colt.

'There ain't no difference between you and them what trade blackhaired scalps to the Mexicans for silver. You and them, getting blood-money for killing.'

Stryker said nothing. In a way, James was right. Most often, he'd collected his reward money with a dead body. But he knew James was trying to rile him.

Tom Easter spoke. 'James. I reckon you came in here to call Matt Stryker out, but it ain't gonna happen in my town. You hear?'

Dolbie James shifted his sharp gaze to meet Tom Easter's cold blue eyes. 'I hear you, Marshal. I reckon you can't be everywhere at once, though.'

'Don't even think about it,' Easter said, his voice knife-edged. 'Prescott ain't no rawhide cowtown or railroad whistle stop. Lots of people here don't even carry weapons. You go to shooting at Matt Stryker and there's no telling who you'd hit. You'll not be gunfighting in my town!'

'Stryker, you've got to leave Prescott sometime. Whatever trail you take outta here, you'll find me facing you down the way. That much you can count on.' James turned his back to

143

Stryker and left the Palace bar, his brothers a step behind.

'Some friends you've got, Matt,' Easter said.

'Should I take them out, Matt?' Tom Hall rubbed his hands down his pants legs as if readying them to grab hold of his big Baker 3-barrel.

'Let it be,' Stryker said, 'but thanks. I'll face the Jameses when the time comes.'

Squirly heard someone rustling around in the stalls while it was still dark. He slipped out from under his blanket and wiggled to the edge of the loft. Whoever it was hadn't lit a lamp. A squeak of leather came from the stall where Injun Jake's appaloosa was. Squirly went to the ladder, quiet as a ferret in his sock feet. The appaloosa snorted.

Squirly backed slowly down the ladder, making no sound. He took shallow breaths. The appaloosa banged against the side of the stall. Someone spoke soft and low to soothe the horse.

A lantern hung on a peg by the tack room door. Squirly liked to smoke and Marshal Stryker gave him and Wildman the makings. Now Squirly dug a lucifer from his pocket. He took special care lifting the lantern chimney. No noise. The appaloosa stomped. He ratcheted up the wick, feeling with his finger to make sure it was right. He scratched the lucifer on the side of the tack room and touched the flame to the wick, then flicked the lever to lower the chimney. Squirly lifted the lantern high.

'Hey you! Whatcha doing with that appaloosa?'

Squirly listened. No sound.

Putting one foot carefully in front of the other, Squirly sidled down the aisle. He wished he'd brought his Dragoon pistol.

'Hey!' Squirly kept the lantern high so he could see. The appaloosa crowded against the near side of the stall. The saddle was gone. Squirly forgot caution. Lantern in his left hand, he charged toward the appaloosa's stall. 'Where's Jake's saddle?' he shouted. 'Come outta there. You some kinda horse thief?'

An arm stabbed out from behind a stall partition and caught Squirly across the throat. He gagged and stumbled, but held on to the lantern. Down on one knee, he tried to turn.

Before he moved more than a couple of inches a hard fist smacked him in the head. Squirly hung on to the lantern. Couldn't set the livery on fire. He grunted when the fist hit, managed to get his feet under him, and lunged. Something glinted in the lantern light and pain blossomed in Squirly's head as a sharp blade split his face open from ear to lip. He tried to holler, but his lips didn't work right.

A scream came from the direction of the ladder. Then running feet pounded. A roar like something incredibly wild, and a thump as bodies met and then crashed into the stall post.

'Friend,' Wildman yelled. Every time his big fists pummelled the attacker, he hollered. 'Friend. Friend. Friend.'

At last the attacker crumpled, knocked senseless by Wildman's fury and mauling fists.

Stryker sat with Catherine de Merode and April, waiting for Bernice the waitress to bring their breakfasts. 'Appreciate you agreeing to stay on with April, Miss de Merode,' he said.

Catherine smiled and the purple in her dark-blue eyes deepened. 'My pleasure, Matthew Stryker. April and I get along famously.'

April nodded enthusiastically. 'My mommy ran away. She maybe thought I was a bad girl and Daddy was a bad man. Catherine says I'm special. Am I special, Uncle Matt?'

Stryker looked at April for a long moment. His lips

curved in a slight smile, but his eyes were full of compassion for this orphan girl. 'Yes, honey,' he said. 'You're special. Very special.'

'Matt.' Tom Easter strode toward their table.

'Good morning, Marshal,' Catherine said.

'Hello, Mr Marshal,' April echoed.

Tom Easter's face said he carried no good news.

'What is it, Tom?' Stryker stood up from the table.

Easter fished a folded paper from his vest pocket and handed it to Stryker.

Stryker unfolded it. He glanced at the paper and then back at Tom Easter. 'I gave this bank draft to Lizzimae Wharton yesterday. Why?'

'Barber Orv had it on him. He tried to ride out earlier.'

'Tried?'

'Yeah. Your friends stopped him. That little guy you call Squirly, he was sleeping in the livery loft.'

'He don't have much money,' Stryker said. 'He mucks out for a place to sleep in the loft. He's honest.'

'Well, Squirly heard someone in the stalls. He snuck down, lit a lantern, and went to see what was going on. Barber Orv cut him pretty bad, but the big one, Wildman, he knocked Orv cold. I got him in jail. He had that bank draft on him. A lotta cash, too.'

Tom Easter shifted uneasily. 'Matt, speak to you private?' He beckoned and walked outside.

Stryker looked at Catherine and April, then followed Easter out.

Tom Easter went a good twenty feet down the porch, leaned on a post, dug the makings from his shirt pocket to roll a quirley, and lit it.

'What's so private, Tom?'

Easter took another draw on the smoke. 'When I found that bank draft and all that cash,' he said, 'I wondered why

Barber Orv had it. Only Lizzimae or Teague would know, so I went over to the Stanton to see them.'

'What'd they say?'

'Lizziemae and Teague are dead,' Easter said. 'Dead in bed, naked, with their throats cut.'

'Barber Orv.'

Easter nodded. 'Your boys did a good turn.'

'Make sure the reward goes to Squirly and Wildman. And they'll get a decent share of the cash, won't they?'

Now all Stryker had to worry about was Dolbie James and his brothers.

17

Down the road Matt Stryker would have to meet Dolbie
James and his brothers over the barrel of a gun. He'd done
gunwork more than once, and he was a careful man. Dolbie
had promised to go face to face with Stryker, and a man with
any kind of gumption kept his word.

Catherine and April did female things, shopping and
such, and Tom Hall'd gone off one some errand or other.

Tom Easter gave the voucher for the reward on Barber
Orv to Squirly, who came to Stryker with it.

'Marshal Easter gave me this here piece of paper,
Marshal, and a fistful of money. What all should we'uns do
with it?'

Stryker led them to Josiah Fish's office. 'Give your
voucher and that cash to Mr Fish, Squirly,' he said. Squirly
did.

'Oh, my. The paper will bring you five hundred dollars.'
Fish counted the bills. He stared straight at Squirly. 'Three
thousand and eighty dollars.'

'Yep. We'uns cotch that cutter man Barber Orv.' Squirly's
face was lopsided with stitches in his cheek. 'That's how
we'uns gots all that money.' Squirly sounded a little proud.

'Mr Fish will keep your money safe, Squirly. And he'll
send you twenty-five dollars a month. That's working man's

wages. You just make sure Wildman gets taken care of. Fair enough?'

'Forever? Twenty-five bucks every month forever?'

Stryker caught Josiah Fish's eye and gave a little nod.

'Yes Mr Squirly. As long as you need it,' Fish said.

'Wildman. Hear that? We got us some money. We don't have to eat them horses' oats any more.'

Wildman smiled. 'Friend,' he said.

Josiah Fish took three tens from the cash Squirly had given him and handed it back. 'For the first month,' he said.

Squirly and Wildman danced a jig around the little room. Stryker watched with his arms folded across his chest, happy the two men would have the wherewithal to live a decent life.

As they left Fish's office, Squirly said, 'Marshal, you reckon me and Wildman could maybe go over to the general store and maybe get some Levis? An' shirts?'

'I reckon you could,' Stryker said.

They parted at the intersection of Gurley and Montezuma. 'Got work to do at the livery,' Squirly said. 'See ya later.'

Wildman said, 'Work.'

Bartholomew Goldfinch stood up when Stryker entered the Jeffery lobby. 'Matt Stryker, I've been waiting for you,' he said. 'We owe you.'

'Hello, Bart. What brings you all the way from Rimrock?'

Goldfinch ducked his head, embarrassed. He dug a wallet from his coat pocket, extracted some bills, and held them out to Stryker. 'Here's the two hundred we owe you, Matt. The two hundred I couldn't pay before.' Then he pulled out a nickel-plated star. 'And here's your badge. We'd sure like you to come back home, Marshal.'

'Rimrock's dying,' Stryker said. 'Where'd you dig up two hundred?'

'People who say Rimrock is dying haven't been there

149

lately. Like I said, the Daggs brothers brought in something like twenty-five thousand woollies. Man named Gerald Hawkins set up a wool depot in town. The bridge over Diablo Canyon is finished so the Western Pacific's building a spur over to Rimrock. The Hashknife outfit choused about fifty thousand head of Texas cows into the country. Their headquarters is Winslow, but they've got a crew located just outside Rimrock. Marshal, the President jumps of a night. Take the star. Please.'

'I'll take the two hundred,' Stryker said. He pocketed the bills.

'And the star?'

Stryker had done everything Stan Ruggart asked of him. His role as personal representative had dribbled down to being long-distance guardian of Stan's daughter April. And Catherine de Merode could handle day-to-day things much better than he. The only thing standing in the way was Dolbie James and his brothers, and Melanie Powers.

'Bart, some men want my hide. I've got to clear that up before I can make plans,' Stryker said.

Goldfinch opened his mouth like he had something more to say, then he shut it again. Matt Stryker wasn't the kind of man you could talk into something. 'Well, all right. The job's yours whenever you want it. Just let us know what you decide to do. I'll be here in Prescott for two more days. If I had an answer to take back, that would help. But I'm not trying to rush you or anything.'

Stryker retrieved his room key from the front desk. 'Thank you, Bart,' he said. 'I'll be in touch.' He climbed the stairs to room 213. Of habit, he stood to one side as he unlocked the door and pushed it open. It was empty. He knocked on the wall separating 213 from 214. No answer. Tom Hall wasn't in.

In fact, Tom Hall, as requested by Catherine de Merode,

had found Melanie Powers and escorted her to Bob Brow's Palace, where Catherine had rented a private room.

Catherine sat in the restaurant with April, who was enjoying her first dish of ice cream since San Francisco, and Shotgun Lou Grimes, who looked uncomfortable without his coach gun.

Tom steered Melanie Powers into the dining room with an iron grip on her arm. 'You stay gentle, girl, and it'll hurt a lot less,' he said. 'Just you listen to Miss de Merode.'

'Good evening, Miss Powers,' Catherine said. 'I've been wishing to have a word with you. I've reserved a private room upstairs. Please join me.'

Melanie fairly hissed. 'I spit in the face of any friend of Matt Stryker. I'll see him dead. He murdered my brother.'

'And your brother was Clayton Powers, correct?'

'Yes!'

'Then, may we repair to the second floor. What I have to say includes your brother.' Catherine shifted her gaze to Tom Hall. 'Mr Hall, would you be kind enough to stay here with April and Mr Grimes?'

The brilliance of Catherine de Merode's smile made Tom Hall do anything she asked. 'Be glad to,' he said, and meant every word.

Catherine led the way. Melanie followed, sure Tom Hall would catch her if she bolted. A round table sat in the center of the private room with six chairs around it, ready for the high-rollers who ordinarily used it. Catherine waved at the chair on the far side. 'If you would be so kind,' she said. She took the near chair.

Melanie plonked herself down. 'What?' Anger flushed her face and she tapped her fingers on the table in frustration. Then she shouted. 'WHAT!'

'I understand you wish to see Matthew Stryker killed,' Catherine said.

'He murdered my brother,' Melanie said.

'Murdered?'

Melanie pouted. 'Shot him dead.'

Catherine let the silence build.

'I took the privilege of looking into your dead brother's affairs,' Catherine said. 'He was not only a robber and a thief, he also killed without compunction.'

'He. Was. My. Brother.'

'Clayton Powers killed at least eleven fellow human beings. Beginning with a clerk at the National Bank of Denver and going on to include a drummer, two railway guards, a stagecoach shotgun rider, a jailer and a deputy, a working girl, and a US marshal.'

Catherine fell silent again.

Melanie opened her mouth, then closed it.

'His last killings were innocents, not saying the other victims were not innocent, but Clayton Powers became involved in a gunfight in Bisbee, and shot a nine-year-old boy and his mother.'

'The kid was an accident,' Melanie said.

'So you know what kind of man your brother was, then?'

'They expelled him from West Point. Everybody there had it in for him.'

Catherine's eyebrows rose. 'West Point?'

In a small voice, Melanie said, 'The oldest son in our family has always gone to West Point.'

'Cashiered, then?'

'Picked on. Harassed. Hazed, just because Papa fought for the South.'

Catherine looked astounded. 'My God. You can't really believe that.'

Melanie jumped to her feet and charged around the table, her fist cocked.

Catherine rose calmly to meet Melanie's rush. She caught

152

Melanie's fist in the palm of her right hand and turned her momentum aside. As Melanie passed, Catherine shoved her with both hands and sent her staggering. Melanie crashed into the wall and fell to her knees. Catherine unbuckled her belt and her skirt fell away. She wore dancer's tights and soft leather shoes.

When Melanie rose she was clutching a small knife. 'Bitch,' she hissed. 'I'll carve your gizzard into little pieces.'

Catherine smiled. 'I think not,' she said. Slowly, she backed away from the table and into an open area.

Melanie stalked her, knife held low and to the side.

Catherine stopped and faced Melanie, her arms hanging naturally, her fingers slightly curled, her feet shoulder-width apart. She still wore the little smile.

'You laughing at me, bitch?' Melanie's voice dripped venom. 'We'll see how much you laugh with your belly slit and your guts dragging on the ground.' Melanie moved in a circle around Catherine, staying some distance away at first, and then slowly narrowing the gap.

As Melanie circled, Catherine turned. The little smile never left her face, but it came nowhere near her eyes.

Melanie dropped her eyes and lifted the knife. She took a big breath and lunged, but Catherine was not there. She'd spun aside and now stood a good ten feet away, smiling. 'Surely you can do better than that,' she said.

Melanie's face contorted. She growled like a wild beast. Spittle formed little patches of cotton in the corners of her mouth. She crouched, knife held low with its cutting edge up. Again she lunged at Catherine, the blade of the knife held horizontal to the floor, waist high, and ready to slash across Catherine's abdomen.

Catherine whirled in time with Melanie's rush, lifting her left leg as she spun and smashing her foot into the side of Melanie's face in a classic savate kick. Melanie went down on

153

all fours, dazed. The little knife skittered across the floor to fetch up against the skirting-board. Catherine scooped the knife up, then delivered a kick to Melanie's ribcage that knocked her breathless and lifted her up and on to her back. Catherine dropped on to the prone woman, her knees pinning Melanie's arms to the floor. Melanie mewled in fear.

Catherine laid the tip of the little knife at the corner of Melanie's left eye. 'Miss Powers, I hear you have a vendetta against Matthew Stryker. Let me warn you. If he is injured or killed by anyone even remotely connected to you, no matter how nebulous that connection, I will personally hunt you down and cut your eyes out. Do I make myself clear?'

The whites of Melanie's eyes showed. She gulped and opened her mouth, but no sound came out. Tears trickled into her ears.

Catherine pricked at the skin next to Melanie's eye. 'Do I make myself clear?'

Melanie couldn't move without pushing the point of the knife into her own eye. Again she opened her mouth. She panted. She swallowed. Catherine raised an eyebrow.

'Yes,' Melanie managed to say.

'I'm sorry. I couldn't quite hear you,' Catherine said.

'Yes,' Melanie said, louder.

'Yes what?'

'Yes you will cut my eyes out.'

'Why would I do a thing like that?'

'If Stryker is harmed.'

'By whom?'

'By anyone connected with me.'

'Good.' Catherine stood.

Melanie sobbed, rolled over on to her stomach, and struggled to all fours. Then, clutching a chair, she pulled herself upright.

'You'll want to take this. It *is* yours.' Catherine held the

154

little knife out, handle first.

Melanie's hand went to her mouth. She stifled a cry, then fled the room, leaving the knife in Catherine's hand.

18

When he got up and thought about what he needed to do that day, Matt Stryker found nothing. Stan Ruggart's affairs were in line. He took a deep breath. A nice quiet job of marshalling in a moribund town like Rimrock, one fighting to make a comeback, might not be a bad thing. He rubbed a hand across the stubble on his face. With the barber gone, he had to scrape his own whiskers off.

Tom Hall waited for Stryker in the lobby, Baker 3-barrel in the crook of his arm. He grinned. 'Cat been clawing your face?' he asked.

Stryker returned the grin. 'Getting rusty at using a straight razor,' he said. 'Damn. Why'd a good barber have to go and start cutting people's throats? A man needs a good shave and two bits is not a bad price to pay.'

'Breakfast?'

'That's what I had in mind. The Old Mill?'

'OK by me.'

Stryker led the way with Tom Hall to his left and half a step behind. The sun was not high enough to bring the late spring heat, and Prescott's mile-high altitude kept briskness in the air. Unbidden, a little smile came to Stryker's face. It felt good to get a job done up right. A bit of a spring came to his steps.

'What's wrong with you?' Tom Hall said. 'You're acting like a kid.'

'Everything Stan asked me to do, done. That's all.'

'Thought maybe you were getting excited about seeing Julie.'

Stryker snorted. 'Must admit she serves a mean cup of coffee,' he said.

Snuffy send word out that he had eggs, so Stryker ordered three, over easy, with sowbelly bacon and fried potatoes. Tom Hall had saleratus biscuits and pebble-dash gravy, then a great big wedge of apple pie.

'Apple pie? The sun just came up,' Stryker said.

'My principle is to get apple pie anytime I can,' Hall said. 'It ain't always gettable.'

Stryker left fifty cents on the table for the breakfasts and a dime for Julie. He strode out of Old Mill with a new lease on life. Dolbie James was waiting for him in the street.

Tom Hall took two quick steps to the right, the Baker 3-barrel still in the crook of his arm.

Dolbie and his two brothers sat on their horses in a line facing the Old Mill, their hands crossed on top of their saddle horns. Morning traffic gave the horses and men a wide berth, but no one stopped to watch the stand-off. Moving wagons and horses and people raised a thin miasma of dust that smelled of dry earth and horse manure.

Mentally, Stryker took stock of his body. The itch from the incision was gone. Doc Craig had removed the stitches some days ago. He'd not been practicing with the Remington, so he wouldn't have his usual sharpness. Couldn't be helped. He faced Dolbie James and waited, hands hanging naturally at his sides.

Injun Jake sauntered up the street and came to a stop three steps to Stryker's left. 'You take Dolbie,' he said. 'I've got Will Roy. Tom can have Rick.'

'Dolbie James!' Tom Easter came up the street with long fast strides. Two deputies trailed him. The lawmen carried cocked Winchesters. 'Dolbie James!'

The James brothers sat motionless.

Easter and his deputies put themselves between Stryker and the Dolbies. 'I told you, James! No gunfighting in my town.'

Dolbie James laughed. 'Tom Easter. Man! You forgetting how to size up a situation?' He turned his gaze back to Stryker. 'You, too, Matt. Tom Hall. Jake. Take a good look. Tell me. What do you see?'

'I ain't got time for riddles, James,' Easter barked.

'Hands on the saddle horns,' Stryker said. 'Winchesters in their boots. Thongs over pistol hammers. No fight here, Marshal.' He folded his arms. 'Take a couple of steps back, Tom. You too, Jake.'

Dolbie nodded. 'That's it, Stryker. That's it.'

'I reckon you came to say something to me, then,' Stryker said.

'We're riding out,' Dolbie said. 'Won't be back.'

'Thought you were all tied up with a family vendetta for that no-good cousin of yours.'

'He was a cousin and he was no good. We figure blood relation's important, but Clayton's sister, the one who called us in on it, says it's all over. So we'll get back to punching cows.' Dolbie started to rein his horse away.

'Since when are you a cowpuncher?' Stryker asked.

Dolbie grinned. 'A man can't make a living with a gun much any more. We got us a little place in the foothills of the Escudilla. Someone said cattle from Scotland do good in high country. We thought we'd get us a Scottish bull.'

'Dolbie, you've been up and up about all of this. Ever find yourself in a jam, you can call on Matt Stryker. I'll be there.'

Dolbie nodded, still smiling. 'I'd enjoy riding with you,

Matt Stryker.' He turned his horse and the three James brothers rode away.

Tom Easter dropped his Winchester into the crook of his left arm. He shook his head and scuffed his boot toe in the dirt of the street. 'Can't imagine Dolbie James punching cows,' he said. 'But then I run into a lot stranger things just about every day.' He shot a sidelong glance at Stryker. 'So, Matt, where does that leave you?'

Stryker took a deep breath before answering. 'On the road to Rimrock, I reckon,' he said.

Stryker came down the stairs from Room 213 with his saddle-bags over his shoulder and his Winchester in his hand. 'Been a pleasure staying here,' he said to the clerk. 'Has Mr Hall come down yet?'

'Mr Hall left sometime before dawn, Mr Stryker. He said you would pay for his room.'

'That's true. Could you have my horse saddled and brought around?'

'Your horse waits out front, sir,' the clerk said.

Stryker raised an eyebrow. 'Really?'

'Yes, sir. Some people out there waiting for you as well.'

'Hmmmmm.' Stryker paid for the rooms.

Four horses stood at the hitching rail. Saif raised his head and whickered when he saw Stryker. A buckboard with a matched team of blacks sat to the side. Bartholomew Goldfinch waited in the shade of the hotel porch. He stepped out to meet Stryker. 'We're ready to hit the road,' he said.

Squirly chimed in. 'We'uns is saddled up, Marshal. An' I got another twenty-five from Mister Fish.'

'Go,' said Wildman. 'Rim. . . .' He ran out of words.

The only one who said nothing was Injun Jake. Jacob Bent. He met Stryker's eyes, but remained silent.

Stryker pulled a star from his vest pocket. 'Bart says

159

Rimrock is coming back. I reckon I'll stay on, keeping the drunks from getting outta line.' He fastened the star to his vest.

He dug out another star and held it out to Jake Bent. 'I'll be needing help in a growing town,' he said. 'I know I can depend on you, Jake. Take the star.'

Jake stayed where he was, leaning against the wall. Eventually he nodded. 'I'll do it, Marshal. But you can be sure I ain't no tame Injun.' He pinned the star to his shirt. 'Let's go,' he said.

A buggy pulled by a chestnut and a bay rolled up beside the hitching rail. Catherine de Merode held the reins and April Ruggart sat beside her. 'If you people are ready, we are ready,' Catherine said.

'Ready for what?' Stryker asked.

'April and I had a long talk,' Catherine said. 'She convinced me it was best that we go with you. She prefers being close to Uncle Matt. I prefer that too. Now. Are you ready?'

'You sure? What about her schooling?'

'Matt Stryker. I am well qualified to teach April everything she needs to know to be a woman, a lady, and a wife,' Catherine said. 'Isn't that why Mr McKendrick and you hired me?'

Stryker couldn't think of a reply. 'Mount up,' he said. 'Jake, you take the lead.'

Jake Bent got on his appaloosa, touched his hat to Matt Stryker, pulled his Winchester from its boot, jacked a round into the chamber, and started down the street.

Stryker waved at Bart Goldfinch to go after Jake, then Squirly and Wildman, followed by Catherine's buggy. Stryker and Saif rode drag. The cavalcade moved east on Gurley Street to Granite Creek, then turned northeast past Whipple Barracks on the road to Rimrock.